A flower unheeded, shall wilt ana aıe,
Under bleak lifestyle, under black skies,
In a gardener's hands, so tender, so fair,
That flower can spout, can love and can care.

Extract from New Blood,
P.A.B

One

Seventeen years.

That was how long had passed since the last time that he had experienced fresh air. Since he had felt the freedom on his wrists rubbed raw from ever-tightening shackles. Since the winds had doted on his thinning dark hair. Since he had worn his own clothes.

"We hereby sentence the defendant, Mister Desmond Ford, to twenty-five years, with the possibility for parole after fifteen."

Seventeen years since those words had passed through him. He still recalled the shock that had gripped his body, the ice cold wrath that ravaged his insides; That had perhaps been one of the last times that he had experienced the truest and rawest emotions that a man could suffer.

The men by his side were uneasy, restless, as they escorted him to that looming iron-wrought gate, the gate that would signal his release. They were not particularly subtle in their discomfort, shuffling and exchanging glances with one another, glances that probably asked "Is this real?"

But no one said anything, the soundtrack of the scene relegated to the light tousling of the winds splitting the grey skies overhead and the crackle of autumnal leaves beneath the boots of the men. How long had it been since such a noise had graced his ears? It must have been as he was walking out of the courthouse, a little shy of two decades ago. When they could go no further, they came to a halt, and there one of the escorts moved further towards the door.

"So, then…" The remaining man pondered with no small amount of deliberation as he stood alongside the now-former inmate. "You going to be taking care of yourself, Mister Ford?"

Ford's response was swift and unemotional, delivering a small, pointed glare that answered any questions that his warden could possibly ask.

"Right, of course…" Awkwardly, he rubbed the back of his head. "Well, you know the drill. Stay out of trouble, see your parole officer once a month, the usual stuff." When he received no verbal reply to this either, he shrugged. "Yeah. I'm sure you do." A sigh, dull and tired, emitted from him and then, he shook his head. "But look, just-"

Before anymore could be said, the front gate racketed open and, taking his case, Ford turned and headed towards it without another glance at the officer. He exchanged only the barest courtesy of a polite nod to the second as he passed him and just like that, he was free. He had crossed from the realm of the prison yard to the car park and the world beyond, saturated with the dim yellows of dead grass. This was the real world.

It didn't appear to be in any better or worse state than it had been when he had left it.

He didn't look over his shoulder, only kept walking as he heard the gates shut behind him. Seventeen years ago, there had been a bus stop nearby; It was time to see if that was still present.

Greenrock Arkansas had been a gorgeous place. Past tense. The kind of place where anyone would be delighted to raise a child. Small, safe and tucked away from the woes of the rest of the world, chipping away at life in its own little corner. None of that had been the case for years now. Even as Desmond looked from the bus window that he rested his head gently on, he could see the deprivation that ran amok, and it only became all the clearer the further that the bus ventured in. What houses were present were dilapidated, with peeling paint and shuttered windows, all punctuated by empty lots, victims of demolition efforts when the rot had simply become too much to sustain anymore. Lawns were unwieldy, a playground for weeds and vast overgrowth, and white picket fences were cracked and fading. It was not entirely devoid of life, for occasionally the bus would pass by a lost, dejected soul shuffling down the faded pavement and the faint glare of glassy eyes could be seen from windows, but otherwise, it was a veritable ghost town.

It wasn't long after entering Greenrock when the bus came to its stop, in the very centre of the town, prompting Desmond to rise from his seat and move across the gantry to the exit, nodding his appreciation to the driver as he did so; He was the only person to disembark there, considering that there were only about five other people on the bus as it was.

Some things never changed.

But Greenrock definitely had.

His boots resting firmly on the pavement, Desmond ran his left hand - his good hand - through his hair as brief spurts of sun peered out from behind the otherwise infinite greyness of the cloud cover. The Greenrock Public Library had once been a sight to behold, a stunning red-brick building that towered over the humble little general stores that surrounded it on all sides, a testament to education and success; Now, the red bricks were fading to a muddy brown, vines and moss crawling up the walls and tapping at the grime-coated windows that could not possibly be seen in or out of. One of the four grand spires of the building had crumbled, another was in the process of doing so and had been very hastily supported with wooden beams. And most of the stores surrounding its little plaza were now long gone, featureless, boarded up icons of nothingness. Still, what time was there to waste? Bringing his head level once again, Desmond adjusted his cowlick so that it no longer fell over his left eye and walked towards the library, the gentle yet faintly imposing breeze threatening to shake his tie loose from his buttoned-up coat.

The glass on the once-grand double doors was as infiltrated with dust as every other window in the place, so much so that Desmond couldn't even hope to look in before he opened the door. And yet, with a memory sharp even after all of those years in a cell, he knew exactly what to expect to see. And he was not disappointed with his own mind. It was more rundown, but this was the lobby that he remembered. From the overhead lighting, archaic and disused, to the dust-coated desk at one end. And then, there was that framed photograph just to the left of the front door.

BLACKMATTER Research Team - July 1989

It had seen far, far better days, but it was still there. Everybody. Doctor Acker, Simon, Lucy, Paul... And in the right of the picture, a young man with dark hair and eyes that were in equal parts piercing and relaxed... And Penny...

He was surprised to see that the photo was still there. Gently, he reached out his left hand, as if to touch it, but caught a hold of his senses and withdrew it back to his side.

He shook his head and carried on his way, taking his focus off the picture for the time being. He had more pressing matters at hand, as he followed the directions towards the archives. There didn't appear to be any librarian nearby, or any patrons either, for that matter. Fine by him, he could get on with what he needed to in peace.

The archives room was one of the smaller ones in the library. This was not to say that it was insignificant, not by any means, but in comparison to the children's section, for example, it was positively dwarfish. It had anything that he could need, though, and it was as he draped his coat over one of the available chairs at the reading table and rolled up his sleeves that he got to work.

1992. October of 1992. That was what he was looking for, in particular. He proceeded with meticulous dedication, straining to read some of the worn and yellowed labels identifying what point in history each section was from. He remembered briefly in his head an old saying of Simon's, that to preserve the past was the ultimate responsibility of each generation. To keep the flame burning, he said. That somewhat naïve optimism almost brought a grin to Desmond's face.

October 1992. There it was. Taking great care, he began to run his finger along the yellowed papers that lined the shelf until he located the exact paper he was looking for. The Greenrock Examiner. Even as he drew closer to what he was searching for, Desmond could feel his heart begin to heave under the pressure. He didn't want to have to dredge this up again, of course he didn't. Not after everything that had happened. But he had to push on. He had made himself a promise seventeen years ago.

October the Twenty-Sixth, Twenty-Seventh… He was getting all the nearer.

Twenty-Eighth, Twenty-Ninth… Thirtieth…

It wasn't there.

Certain that he had missed something, Desmond moved back to the Twenty-Seventh and leafed through the copies from there. No. He hadn't missed it. October the Thirty-First's issue wasn't there. It went straight from the Thirtieth to November First, the latter of which contained some story about a rare species of bird found roosting in the town.

"The hell…" He muttered to himself, biting down on his bottom lip very softly as he took a step back. The facts couldn't be denied. The copy of the Greenrock Examiner from October Thirty-First should have been there. Simon had told him specifically that he had donated it. Had he been lying? No. No, Simon would have understood the importance of the matter. He wouldn't have been so flagrant.

So then, where the hell was it?

There was no denying the fact that it wasn't there. Thirtieth, First… Second… No head nor tail of the Thirty-First.

Resisting the urge to kick the shelf, Desmond took another step back. This was a roadblock, to be sure, but he was far from out of the fight just yet. He had been stewing on this plan for nearly two decades, of course he had considered the possibility, as unlikely as he had hoped it to be.

Phone book. There had to be a phone book somewhere in the library. And so, casting his final gaze at the shelf of newspapers, he took off in search of it.

It took him half an hour and two different sections of the library, but he finally managed to come across one, a heaving, dusty volume that was listed as being from 2005. Four years ago. Not ideal, but it was better than one from 1992, and Desmond reasoned that he probably wasn't going to find one that was any newer. Beggars could not be choosers. And so, he took a seat and began to pour through it. Name after name blended into his mind, swirling around in infinite nothingness. No sign of a Simon living in Greenrock, or any Lorde for that matter. Regardless, he kept flipping through. If not Simon, maybe anybody else. There had to be someone who he remembered still living in this Godforsaken town. Anyone at all.

Stanton, Paul.

There it was. Even as he turned to the page, the name immediately leapt out at him. Paul Stanton. Surely, that had to be him. Still living in Greenrock and with a registered number. Would he be cooperative, though? Desmond had not the faintest clue, but it was worth a try. With a swift, deft motion, he tore the page out of the book and placed it back where he had found it. It wasn't as if anybody would be looking for the phone book - or indeed, entering the library - anytime soon.

 Exiting back out into the plaza, it proved to have developed no further life since Desmond had left it, be it from the fountain in the centre that had not spurted water in years and was now left clogged with dry leaves, or the abandoned pathways that allowed him easy access without having to encounter anybody. A few people could be seen on the other side of the road, milling about as if they weren't quite alive, but that was about the extent of it. Desmond quickly checked his watch, confirming that it was only nine in the morning, still. He supposed he couldn't expect much of the town's mostly aged population to be up and about at this time. Either way, it benefited him, since the phone booth on the corner of the street was free.

 It was a disgusting thing, caked in graffiti and with an overwhelming stench of sweat and rot that hit Desmond from the second he stepped inside and only exacerbated itself as he shut the door. The phone itself was not in the best of states and it did not help that he had to constantly look back and forth between it and the number in order to enter it. The rotary cylinder was stiff and felt as if it had some sort of gum stuck in the mechanism, but he did manage to fight against it, inputting the number and picking up the phone - which was sticky to the touch - before bringing it to his ear.

 It dialled for a while, a shrill series of clicks and bleeps that threatened to split Desmond's ear canals into pieces, and for a moment, he did come to believe that he wasn't going to get any kind of response. But he kept ringing and finally, it did come through, the dialling cutting short to be replaced by the faint static of background noise. After a moment of awkward silence, Desmond spoke first.

 "Hello?"

 "Hello?" The voice on the other end came back, a frail, elderly and above all else tired tone that sounded as if the owner was moments away from hanging up. "Stanton household."

 So he had called the right place. "Right. Is this Paul Stanton speaking?"

 A short pause. "Yes. That is me."

"Good, good." Desmond nodded, leaning against the glass walls of the booth. "It's Des."

The period of silence that followed was long and deafening in its anticipation. He then spoke again. "Hello?"

"Ford." Stanton eventually said, with a new tone creeping into his voice to join the others. A slithering distaste, dislike even. "So you're out of prison."

"I was just released today, yes." He answered pleasantly. "But please, I don't have much time for small talk. I need-"

"You need?" Stanton spat back. "You say you need something? What the hell could you possibly need from me?"

"Paul-"

"Listen, Ford. I'm not particularly happy at the thought of talking to you after what you did."

"What I-" Desmond began repeating before he fell into silence, quickly finding a way to cut back. "Have you forgotten what O'Connor did? We were all in trouble long before-"

"Don't try to patronise me." Paul retorted. "We had things under control. And you-"

Now, it was Desmond's turn to interrupt. "Under control?" He hissed, feeling the frustration swell up in him. "Five people were dead, you call that 'under control'?"

"What happened was a tragedy, but don't pretend for a second that you didn't make things worse." Now the anger was coming into Stanton's voice. "We had a good thing going. By all means, Icarus was a success. But you just couldn't let the results speak for themselves."

Desmond's left eye twitched. He wasn't going to get anything out of this, was he? The moments passed as his head spun and he took a few deep breaths. "I'm not going to argue with you about this, Stanton. I'm looking for Simon."

"Lorde? He's long gone, I can tell you that much."

Long gone? "What, is he dead?"

"As far as you're concerned, he might as well be." And then, the line was down. Stanton had hung up. Desmond was left standing there in a state of utter confusion. He had not expected the talk to be smooth, but for it to be so completely disastrous as that? He was sure that they would have understood. Acker was insane, but were they not any better? Had it really only been he and Simon who had found any kind of problem with Icarus?

Suddenly, he became explicitly aware of just how tired he felt. His legs were stiff and his arms no better. Perhaps it would be for the best if he... Well, he didn't even know what to do from here.

Biting down on his bottom lip, he stepped out of the booth and back into the sweet release of the fresh air. Well, what now? He supposed that the best idea right now would be to get a roof over his head. That shouldn't prove all too difficult, for he did know of a place, although whether it was still open or not could be anybody's guess.

Two

Even back twenty years ago, when Greenrock had still been in a semi-reasonable state, the little motel on the edge of the town still had not been. It was once the exception, the one part of the area that felt decrepit and mostly lifeless; As much as Desmond would have liked to believe that it would remain the exception and flip itself around with the town's worsening fortunes, now it just belonged in the scenery far more.

For as uncooperative as the receptionist was, he did eventually manage to procure a key for a room on the first floor and it was relatively cheap at that. He certainly got what he paid for. The room was tiny in the purest sense of the word, with a stiff-looking bed pressed tight into the wall and a few basic appliances directly opposite from it. That was really it and there was not much floor space to walk about in. A window sat just above the bed, but so caked with filth was it that one couldn't hope to look out of it and as a result, a dim, murky shadow was cast over the entire room. Flicking on the light did not help matters, as it was a single, flickering, naked bulb that hung over the bed and swung dangerously as it buzzed and heaved to stay on.

Releasing his grip on his bag, Desmond sat down on the mattress, which was as hard as one would expect from looking at it. He had seen and felt better. In fact, he reckoned that he would probably have been happier back in his cell. He allowed himself a brief bitter chuckle as he glanced up at the stained ceiling. Absurd. There he was, feeling nostalgic for prison. He must have gone completely stark-raving mad. It couldn't be denied that he had been living in better conditions just the previous night. What a thought that was.

He realised that he would do well to take his mind off that topic, so he got back to business, stroking his chin gently as he thought. Without the newspaper plan, he was going to have to find an alternate way to get into the facility. Obviously, just leaving it be was no option at all, but if he couldn't get past the front doors, then what could he do? Theoretically, the facility was abandoned, but with BLACKMATTER, that meant very little at all. Just waltzing in was not going to be an option. But without any official method of getting inside…

Desmond had once known a man when in prison, who had gone by the name of Farrell. This man had told him that everywhere on earth had its entrances, and one just had to think outside of the box when looking for it. Now, Farrell was a child killer, so Desmond wasn't going to put much stock into what he had said, but even so, it gave him food for thought.

If he was going to think outside of the box, then he would have to actually go down and take a look at his choices. But first and foremost, he was in severe need of a shower, his joints stiff and screaming for some sort of relief.

In the end, the meagre shower in his room did not provide any such relief. It was stuck to freezing cold and would not warm up no matter how long he left it running for and the shower itself was an enclosed, narrow, claustrophobic space that was highly reminiscent of the phone booth and was only made worse by the worrying stains on the walls that Desmond did everything in his power to not come into contact with. Yet another area in which prison had this place thoroughly beaten. Even still, it was something of a relief to run the water through his hair, to feel his joints loosen up just a little, as much as he probably could have hoped for. He was sceptical of just how much it *cleaned* him, per se, but it just about did the job. Mostly.

As Desmond had a very limited knowledge of how the town's transit system functioned very much, if at all, nowadays, he instead elected to walk to the

BLACKMATTER facility. It would be a lie to call the walk pleasant for, although the fresh air was something to behold for someone so acquainted with prison, the sights left a lot to be desired and that was being generous. Greenrock truly had gone to pot, there were no two ways about it. All in all, the walk took him about half an hour, to cross the entirety of the town to the southern outskirts, where the facility rested, and by the time that he reached his destination, he truly felt each and every step.

BLACKMATTER's facility was about what one would expect from a supposedly abandoned laboratory on the far side of a deprived town. White, metallic walls that were stained with age and abuse, wild untamed grounds with weeds that claimed the parking lot for themselves and all surrounded by a high wire fence, topped with barbed edges and adorned with all kinds of signs warning against trespassers. It very much looked as if it hadn't been touched since 1992.

 Looking around, Desmond strived to look as casual as possible, keeping his hands in his coat pockets and walking around the side of the fence, scanning it for any kind of hint of an entrance. It didn't appear to be electrified, so that was one thing, but in equal stride, there was no sign of any gaps or openings, be they intentional or otherwise. What chances did he have of scaling it? While it didn't appear impossible, he told himself it was worth keeping in mind that he was closer to fifty than thirty and as much as he had kept his body active in prison, he still had his limitations, chief among them being the fact that he could only reliably use one hand. With all that in mind, the wire at the top could prove to be problematic.

He did find, near the back corner of the building, a door in the fence that from the looks of it, required some form of key. Just to test it, he rattled the handle. Nothing at all. Of course it wasn't going to be that easy. He began to feel somewhat frustrated. This wasn't some high-end defence that he was dealing with, this was the kind of quickly-erected fencing that they used on construction sites to temporarily keep undesirables out at night time. It wasn't difficult to get through, not theoretically at least. And there he was, struggling. Very frustrating.

Okay, he just needed to think a little more about this. He was entirely correct, it was a flimsy little chain link fence. He could come up with *some* way to deal with it, without much of an issue at all. After all, he hadn't come with thoughts of getting in immediately, this was simply to survey the area. And survey, he had. Of course, even after that, he still wasn't sure how he would get into the actual building with Simon's assistance, but he would cross that bridge when he came to it. For now, the fence was the most pressing matter at hand. And he probably needed somewhere better to ruminate on it all.

Personally, he was surprised that Greenrock had any cafés at all, anymore and although it was not the one he had always enjoyed back in easier times, he had managed to come across one that he decided would be a good place to sit and think on his next move. Better than the motel room, at least. It was a little family-owned joint, near the centre of town, with the library just a block away and, thankfully, the place was empty enough that he had no trouble getting a seat by a window. He liked to sit by windows when at a restaurant or anything of the like and even he knew not the reason why; Maybe it provided an easy escape point in the case of an emergency.

Before he could think about anything else though, he was going to have to wrap his head around this menu. There appeared to be about eight hundred different types of coffee, none of which he had ever heard of in the past. Had the world of caffeine really changed so much in seventeen years? How difficult was it to get a basic coffee?

Eventually, he did manage to place an order with a young girl who looked like she would rather be anywhere else in the world at that moment and was able to settle down, taking a moment to adjust himself in the seat to be a tad more comfortable. He didn't exactly manage that, for the wood of the seating was probably about as old as he was and had aged about as gracefully, but he came close enough to something vaguely approximating comfort.

At the very least, the service could not be complained about, as he received his drink within just a few minutes, certainly less than ten. As far back as he could recall, that made for rather decent serving time. Then again, it wasn't as if there were all too many people to hold up the wait time.

Regardless, he was quite happy to sip away at the surprisingly not lukewarm drink as he briefly consulted the complimentary paper that someone had left on the table. It was dated from a couple of days ago and the story wasn't anything special, just a brief overview of someone from a neighbouring town who had been caught with cocaine. Desmond permitted himself a light smirk at this. Clearly, he was not the only one stuck in the eighties. And, although lacking substance, it allowed him to keep his eyes busy as he sipped, which he was more than appreciative of.

But of course, as he drank, his thoughts shifted away from the paper and more towards what he should do next. The way that he saw things, scaling that fence was likely out of the question. As far as he remembered, there was an old hardware store down near the eastern end of the town, and assuming that it was still open, which was a major case of wishful thinking, then perhaps he could get his hands on a pair of bolt cutters. If he couldn't go over, he could always go right through. The question was, could he even operate them with only one hand to spare?

Whatever his thoughts may have been, they were suddenly diverted by the presence of a new figure, someone sitting down right in front of him at the very same table. This gave Desmond pause for thought for a moment. "Hello?" He asked the intruder with a raised eyebrow.

To say that the man stood out would be an understatement. He was adorned entirely in black, black-tinted glasses, a black overcoat and a black formal sweater beneath, and his hair, although also black, was flecked with grey at the temples. This grey was the only possible indicator of his age, for everything else about him seemed oddly ethereal, from his indistinguishable build to pale skin that contrasted almost comically against the darkness of his attire.

"Desmond Ford." The man nodded politely.

That was when he edged up even more. He didn't get where this was going yet, but he was on high alert, his entire body tensed. "And who's asking?"

"That isn't relevant." The man replied briskly, taking a pen from his breast pocket and tapping it off the wooden surface of the table in a near-hypnotic motion. "I know who you are and that is what matters. Moreover, I know what you are. What you're doing here."

Desmond felt his entire body run cold, and yet he fought to keep his voice even. "I don't pretend to understand what you're talking about. I'm an ex-con, visiting my home town. Is there anything so startling about that?"

The man leaned back in his chair and Desmond could tell that behind the glasses, his eyes were scanning the rest of the room. "Maybe not. Not if this was your home town. But I know that isn't true. I know that you were born in Arizona. You moved here in the early eighties. You moved here for your job." He looked back and his stare was an intense beam of scrutiny. "A job that no longer exists. You have no reason to be here. No ordinary reason. So, why return here, to this reminder of the things you've done?"

Desmond didn't immediately respond. He couldn't. His mind was bursting with a million questions, one of the main ones being just who this was. And he didn't have the faintest answer. Something about this man looked oddly familiar, but… God, he felt sluggish. Heavy.

"We can't have you causing any problems." He continued as he moved to stand up. "So I took the courtesy of adding something a little stronger to your drink. You should sleep off the coffee, calm yourself down. And when you wake up, perhaps you'll be in a better state to make the correct decision."

Desmond wanted to speak. He wanted to lash out, curse at the man. But, as that figure stood and went to leave the café without another word, he already knew that it was a lost cause. Whoever this was, whatever his end goal was… In that moment, none of it mattered, none of it at all. Dammit. With a dull groan, he pulled himself to his feet and already, it was evident just how much of an effect that was being waged on him. Even in spite of his shower no more than three hours ago, he was stiff and more than that, heavy. His bones ached, the entirety of his body did.

Taken aback by his state, he found the need to support his wiry frame by resting his hand on the table. This was new to him, all new and terrifying. In prison, when someone wanted to attack you, they were upfront and simple about it. He had been outright ambushed, once, but never poisoned. What even was it? From the way that the man had talked about it, he doubted it was entirely lethal, for all that meant. The thought only really reassured him in the way that a starving man took refuge in the sight of a prowling tiger, set to end his misery.

As he stumbled towards the door, the young woman who had served him approached him once again, her large, pretty eyes bulging with concern. "Are you alright, sir?" She asked, clearly noting just how winded he appeared.

"I'm quite… I'm quite alright, dear." He cringed at his own words. Dear? He was forty-five, not eighty-five and in spite of his current state, he wasn't a doddering old grandfather just yet. "Your concern is… Appreciated, but I'm fine." Even he could acknowledge just how raspy voice sounded. His head was spinning, pounding. He just wanted to get the hell out and lie down, a task that seemed all the more difficult with each second that passed. Regardless, he managed to dismiss the girl from offering any more help. Now, he just needed to make it to the door.

How hard could it possibly be?

It was simple. One foot in front of the other, rinse and repeat. A basic rhythm that he could keep up without much effort, surely. Deep breaths, one foot, the other foot. He pushed away from the table and kept this pattern ringing in his mind, refusing to let go of it. The door was coming closer. Or was it? With how his vision swam, it was somewhat difficult to tell.

Even in his addled state, he knew that he had to reach the entrance at one point, for he felt the coolness of the handle and pushed it open, flinging himself out into the cold air of the outside, where there was absolutely no trace of the man to be seen, not that this surprised him at all. The atmosphere played on his sweat-racked skin, bringing out goosebumps and shivers that he could barely take notice of.

Now… Now, he just had to get back to the motel.

Just wonderful.

Three

He didn't know how he managed it, perhaps whatever god rested up above was simply in a playful mood, but however it happened, Desmond was able to get as far as his bed back in the motel, where he collapsed down and, caring not for the toughness of the mattress of the roughness of the sheets, he felt sleep come to grasp him, and he was all too willing to accept it.

When his eyes closed and the world around him faded, he saw himself. It was as if he were an audience watching a film, viewing his own body from the third person, a younger body, with a face distorted by his mind yet undeniably still him. And he watched himself travel down a corridor. A corridor of gleaming white, a corridor that he recognised very well, even as it had been seventeen years since he had stepped foot in it. He walked at a frantic pace, almost running, tie flapping behind him and by his side, another man. A man both taller and stockier than Desmond.

"Are you really sure about this?" Simon Lorde protested, his voice somewhat strangled by exasperation as he kept up the pace with his friend. "Don't you reckon you should calm down, take a breather?"

"Calm down?" Desmond's younger form laughed bitterly as he continued on his warpath. "Calm down, after five people are already dead? That's what you want me to do?"

"I know, okay? We're all freaking out about this, but Acker-" Suddenly taking more initiative, Simon broke forward and tried to block Desmond from going any further, grasping the man's shoulder. "Listen to me, okay? Acker's feeling it as hard as the rest of us are, we're all in this together."

And that was when Desmond realised that this wasn't just a dream, a concoction of his depraved mind mixed with whatever drugs had been pumped into him; This was a memory. And he knew the exact words that were coming next, even as his younger self regarded Simon with what could only be interpreted as a harsh glare, part of the distortion eating away to reveal the thin scowl that overtook his mouth.

"Acker is insane."

With those words, he tried to move past, but Simon maintained his barrier. "Jesus Christ, Des, if you don't calm it, I'm gonna call Bobby down here, I swear."

"Oh, Bobby?" Desmond muttered sarcastically. "Whatever will I do about that? I'll have to start a brisk jog to outrun *him*."

"Hey, come on, that's not fair." In spite of the situation, Simon couldn't help but let out a dry little smirk. He quickly corrected it with a shake of his head. "You need to cool off."

"I'll cool off *after* I've spoken to Acker." Desmond insisted, pushing around his friend and turning the corner, the observational view of the whole scene following him down the corridor.

"Hey!" Simon shouted, trying to run after him. "Penny's in there too, you know." It was an attempt to calm him down, to stop him in his tracks. But just for a moment there, the veil covering younger Desmond's face lifted and the expression of pure, unfiltered rage sent chills down the spine of his present self.

"I know." He growled through grit teeth, coming to a heavy sealed door at the end of the hall and violently producing his key card from his coat pocket, slamming it down through the scanning slot. It took a moment for the electronic doors to part.

And when they did, all hell broke loose.

Desmond knew what was coming next, he knew it all too well, but like an old projector reel left in the elements for decades, the memory had corrupted and what he was greeted with past that door was something he had not anticipated at all. A howling mass of stroke-inducing colours, of tortured screams and wailing cries. Everything was flashing too fast to get a proper read on, shapes vaguely resembling human beings passing into view before passing right back out again, all overlapped with the absolutely unthinkable cries of a young child. It was like Pandora's Box had opened up and armageddon had been unleashed upon the scapes of his mind. Every bit as horrifying as it was utterly horrifying, there was no solace at all to be felt. Just a cold, unending nightmare.

And then, it ended.

Desmond found his eyes force themselves open, staring off at the stained wall that ran adjacent to his bed. His entire form was hot, wrapped in sweat and shot nerves. It took several moments for him to even adjust to what was going on, and longer still for him to content himself with the fact that he had safely returned to the world of consciousness.

Dammit. This shouldn't have been so startling. In those seventeen years in a dim concrete cell, he had become far from a stranger to the terrors of the eve. But this was different. Altogether more disturbing than the usual affair, in a way that he simply was not used to. It took a while before he found the strength to haul his body into an appropriate sitting position on the bed, feet gracing the cold floor. It took another second for him to realise that he was actually trembling. Something about that had instilled more fear in him than anything else in his life had. Maybe just shy of the day itself...

He shook his head. Whatever that gentleman at the café had intended, he was to surely find himself sorely disappointed. All that this had achieved, outside of faintly disturbing Desmond, was emboldening his resolve. His bizarre fever dream had convinced him of one thing and that was that he needed to continue on, he simply could not afford not to, not with the unimaginable costs that came with BLACKMATTER's ambitions.

But headstrong, Desmond was not, at least not to the point of blindness to the reality of the situation. The man who had visited him made his intentions clear. Somebody did not want him looking around the facility. They probably wanted him gone from Greenrock as soon as possible and yet they were not willing to simply kill him at this stage. Perhaps it was too much of a hassle to risk if they thought he could still be reasoned with. Any normal man would surely take their warning to heart and drop any scheme that they may have been hatching. This was Desmond Ford, however, and his mission, a mission built up in his head over seventeen years, would not be dismantled so easily. Even so, he knew now that caution was key. No doubt from the moment he stepped foot outside of the motel room, he would be watched. If he went anywhere near the facility, if he made the slightest suspicious move, they would be on him, and they were unlikely to be as forgiving as they had been the first time.

Was that even the case? Was this just the disordered ramblings of a paranoid mind, already shaken by the nightmare?

No. There had to be something deeper to it, that was a simple fact of the matter. Someone had dispatched the man in all black to confront Desmond and that much was no fantasy.

Or was it? Had that even really transpired? Maybe it had all been some absurd dream, perhaps he had been asleep from the moment he arrived at his room…

He brought his hand up to hold his temple, as if in fear that it may split apart. He was second guessing himself, and that was something that he could not allow by any means. Even if all of that was the case, he would be best to go ahead under the assumption that the threat was true. Or was-

"Jesus Christ." He muttered to himself in a bitter tone. He really had to get a hold of himself, stop raising potential flaws and alternatives with every thought he bred. He was being watched, it was as simple as that and he would not hear anything else to the contrary for the time being, especially not from his own mind.

With all of that said, it still left the question of what to do next. The previous day, he had made allusions to a hardware store… Something to get through the fence. Yes, that was it. But were he being watched, then such a plan was suicide, particularly if he approached anything even resembling a tool shop. That would raise alarm bells in the head of his stalker in every possible direction. To be careful in his next step was the name of the game.

From the window, as grime-coated as it was, Desmond couldn't see anybody who appeared to possibly be watching over him. Or anybody at all for that matter. But that meant very little in the grand scheme of things, unable to prove or disprove anything in particular. More than anything else, he needed to find a way to test it.

It was time, he reckoned, for a walk.

The new day proved Greenrock to be no more active than it had been the previous. As Desmond made his way through the town, he maybe encountered one person every ten or so minutes, a far cry from how he remember things back in the eighties; At that time, it was hard not to run into somebody and quite often that somebody would have something pleasant to say. No such chance nowadays. It was just him and his thoughts and the lightly bitter cold of Arkansas autumn. His hands remained deep into the pockets of his coat, so as to try and negate the effects of the chill just a little. Perhaps he should invest in some gloves.

On more pressing matters, he couldn't appear to identify anybody who may have been following him, as he used shop windows, dark puddles on the sidewalk and the flash of the occasional passing car to search behind him without appearing all too suspicious. He wasn't sure how successful this endeavour was, but right now, he couldn't afford to take all too many risks.

As he walked, he kept his mind alive with various acts of scheming. Once he was past the fence, however he would manage that, his next item on the agenda would be to actually get into the facility proper. How he could do that with his original plan scarpered was anybody's guess. While he had no doubt that BLACKMATTER was continuing to use the building, it was undeniable that they were certainly having to keep it under wraps, maintain the façade of the facility as decrepit and utterly abandoned. Perhaps there would be something there that could assist him. It was a big if, but better than nothing. Regardless, he would have to figure it out once he was actually on the scene.

Then, came the issue of what to do once he was inside. And this was something that he already had a shining answer ready for. Collect all the documentation that he needed, files, notes, anything at all. Release them to the public at large, to as many papers and two-bit journalists as he could find. Someone, somewhere, would be brave enough or insane enough to get it published. And then, BLACKMATTER simply could not hide for any longer. That hopefully wouldn't prove too difficult, assuming that the sharpness of his mind was enough to remind him accurately of where most of what he could use was stored. That, he reckoned, could be good enough.

And then, he caught it. Out of the very corner of his eye, so subtle that he very nearly paid it no heed whatsoever. But something about it prompted a double take. He fell still, glancing into the window of the computer repair store just beside him (people went to actual stores to repair computers, now? Just how popular were they in the twenty-first century?) Sure enough, he saw it again. A subdued vehicle, all black and entirely innocuous, going past him and turning at the corner. Too innocuous, in fact. That car… Desmond could swear that he had seen it before. Even in the distorted reflection and as it was disappearing around the aforementioned corner, he managed to catch onto a portion of the licence plate.

508.

The number stuck in his mind like a tumour. He wouldn't let go of it. He was going to keep that little detail very much in his head. And so, with that logged, he kept going, now with a newfound determination creeping up his back.

Sure enough, no more than five minutes later, it passed him again. Black sedan. 508 on the licence. It was circling.

Stalking.

Surprisingly, even to himself, the feeling that he got from this was… Elating, almost. Not quite that far, but to at least have something resembling a confirmation that his worries were legitimate was certainly something of a relief, in a roundabout sense. Now that he knew the answer for good, he could do something about it. The question was now, what to do, exactly?

He didn't even really think as he pushed open that door and stepped into the computer store. It was a cramped, dusty little place, still in operation, but probably not facing the greatest business possible. Then again, did any shop in Greenrock do well? At the far end, behind a small counter, stood a particularly bored-looking teenager and from the looks of things, there didn't appear to be any form of closed circuit television. Behind the boy, there was a weak wooden door labelled as being for employees only.

Right. Now, what to do… Desmond's mind ran quickly, going through a hundred ideas a second. That door had to lead to some sort of back entrance, surely. Whoever was in the black sedan would most likely be waiting for him to come back out of the store, so if he took the other direction, then theoretically…

Of course, then there was the matter of just how to do it. The teen was inattentive, but not *that* inattentive and the space was far too narrow to even consider slipping past unnoticed. Slowly, looking as if he was a browsing customer, he walked down the aisle, rubbing his chin gently. Computers had definitely changed a lot in twenty years. Smaller, more compact, sleeker in design. It was a bit of a shock, to say the least. Even more breathtaking was the price point. They weren't negligible prices, he would give them that much, but when one considered how these things used to cost… To think that they were so easily affordable for the common consumer. He shook his head with a dry little grin, nearly losing himself in the sight. Unimaginable.

For a moment, he looked back up to the counter, then down to the stock again. There only seemed to be that one kid there… And that sparked a little idea in the back of his mind. On the very bottom shelf, there was a little personal computer. And the price tag on it was clearly flaking.

"Um, excuse me?" He called, straightening himself up and directing his gaze to the employee. "Could I have a bit of help, please? He used his most pleasant possible tone, which probably clashed a tad with his usually gruff manner of speaking.

The boy rolled his eyes and groaned a little, but he did come over. That was step one, at least. He came into the aisle and stood there, looking like he wanted to get back to his counter as soon as possible, even as he asked "You good, Sir?"

"Well, yes, I was just taking a look at these..." Desmond nodded as he bent down to where the small little portable computer sat. "I was wondering, would you have many of these in stock? I'm just thinking, this is exactly the kind of thing that I need, but I can't appear to find any kind of price. Would you have any insight on the matter?"

The teen was apathetic. "Huh. It really isn't there, is it?"

"No. I really have looked all over. It is for sale, isn't it?"

"Uh... Maybe, I guess. I could go look in the back for you, real quick."

The back? Not ideal, but presumably that would get him out of the store front for the time being, give some breathing room. "If you wouldn't mind, that would be wonderful, thank you very much."

A long, drawn-out sigh followed. "Fine. I'll be back in a couple minutes."

"No need to rush." Desmond smiled politely as he watched the kid withdraw through that door at the back and disappear into nothingness. Well, that was one step closer, at least. How long the gentleman would be in the back wasn't certain, so it would probably be an idea to move quickly. Pushing up to the desk, he tried to look as casual as he possibly could as he walked around the counter, reaching the door. From there, he deliberated for just a few moments before he opened up the door, just by a crack, and glanced through.

He saw out into a narrow hallway, characterised by humble wallpaper and ignored cardboard boxes. Directly opposite from where Desmond stood was another door and this was open by quite a margin, giving a view into what looked like a storeroom of sorts. Sure enough, the kid was there, and he had his back to the door.

He knew that if he waited any longer, he would only find more reasons to hesitate and so, he went for it, pushing open the door into the hallway as far as he could without drawing much attention and flattened his body to the frame, slipping through slowly and carefully.

This was absurd. Everything that he had been through, and was surely about to be through in the coming future, and yet there he was, heart practically beating out of his chest because of a simple teenager in a rundown little electronics store. It was difficult to keep himself steeled. But regardless, he got through and all without attracting any attention.

Now, he just had to find a way to leave the building through a back door.

Four

In the end, once he did make his way outside, it took
about an hour and a half to get from the store back to the
facility, an hour and a half of keeping up utmost caution,
of checking every corner, ducking into any degree of
shade he could find. To anyone watching, he most likely
looked like a completely paranoid lunatic, but he didn't
allow that to daunt him much, for it wasn't as if there
were many people present anyway. As far as he was
aware, he had not seen the black sedan again, so that
provided him with some degree of hope that he had been
able to get away with it.

And so, finally, he stood outside the BLACKMATTER
facility once again. It really did hold a certain power to
it, casting a spell over him just as he looked it over.
Perhaps a lot of that came from the memories; The
memories and the knowledge of what was going on
within those fragile-looking walls.

One immediate problem was that in his bedraggled
state, he had decided not to risk going to the hardware
store. In fact, he didn't even pass it. It was most likely
long closed anyway, judging from the state of much of
the rest of the town. That meant no tools. But he was

there now, and without risk of being caught by his stalker once again, he would just have to make do. With one good hand. What could possibly go wrong?

He shook his head. There had to be something. It was a flimsy little wire fence, it couldn't be impenetrable. There had to be some sort of weakness, something that he could surely exploit to get beyond it. So he searched. The front facing wall was, as expected really, entirely lacking in any form of entryway, official or otherwise. Much was the same for both of the two adjacent to it . And as for the back, there was that aforementioned door built into the gate, which once again was quite rigidly locked up, but aside from that, he could see little. He got down to a crouch, feeling the somewhat unpleasant sensation of the damp mud of the field lapping at his coat, and examined as close as he could, resting his hand on the wireframe to keep his body steady. And from this, after what must have been about five minutes of careful inspection, he saw something.

It was subtle, so much so that most people would certainly have glossed over it, but for a man in a state as desperate as Desmond, things were slightly different, he was more attentive and through this, he took note of a small segment at the bottom of the fence that was turned up ever so slightly, the silver wire caked in mud and twisted to face the grey skies overhead. It must have been some sort of rabbit or something along those lines burrowing its way out. Obviously far too small for any grown man, or indeed any child. But it was a start.

He brought his hand to that patch of the fence and, testing the waters, pulled it on, lifting it just a little and leaving a larger gap beneath. Another harder pull revealed even more. It still wasn't what could be called a comfortable fit under any delusions out there, but it was getting closer. Another couple of tugs and it was nearly up to his knee from his crouching position, and from there, it would budge no longer. It would seem that he had exerted this method of potential entry.

It was certainly due to be a tight fit, but it appeared to be far from out of plausibility's realm. It was the best that he was going to get, at least. Now, came the miserable part.

Sighing to himself, Desmond got down to his knees, instantly feeling the mud seep into his trousers, and softly lowered the rest of his body so that he was in a crawling position, eyes just barely level with the top of the hole he had created. Uncomfortable *and* undignified. What a combination. But if such things were off putting to him, then he would have quit long ago. So, he cast away his pride and began to crawl.

He had quite possibly misjudged just how tight it was. Even with his arms tucked as close into his sides as he could possibly manage, there was just barely enough space to pass through, and doing so was not without issues, as his body rotated awkwardly, prickling at the edges of curled wires that seemed to reach out, stroking his sides and face. For a moment, he felt like he was a child again, exploring the woods behind the family home with Reggie the ever-reliable sheepdog. But today, there was no dog to stay by his side. And there was little sense of wonder, either. Just mud and plain grey steel.

It felt like hours had passed, but in what was probably far closer to thirty seconds, Desmond managed to force himself through, a loose strand of the metal wire catching his cheek as he did so and drawing a thin red line across it. When his chest touched fractured concrete, that was when he knew he was through, and so, he started to pull his body back up.

His cheek had not been the sole victim of the fence's ferocity. Little nicks and cuts raged across his body, tiny little pricks and tears in his clothes that were, although not debilitating, certainly irritating. But all of that was largely irrelevant; He was through, he was past the fence, and for the moment, that was all that truly mattered to him.

The building certainly looked more imposing up close, surprisingly tall for what it was and mounted with not a single visible window. Natural light was not a phrase that Doctor Acker or any of the researchers had been altogether acquainted with. In the decades since last he had entered, it had only grown all the more hostile. The parking lot was completely empty, the yellow marker lines faded into the tarmac, and the dumpster around the side was positively overflowing, the contents within long forgotten and with no hope of being collected any time soon.

It certainly looked abandoned.

But was it truly? Desmond had his suspicions, but they would only really be answered once he found his way inside. And so, he made a line for the front doors. To the shock of absolutely no one, least of all him, they were locked up tight, secured with a heavy padlock and with a sign pinned to the front proclaiming the building's closure. The card scanner had been ripped directly out of the wall. In an odd way, this provided Desmond with a sort of relief; That newspaper, which had held within it his old key pass, would not have been of any use anyway. At least, none when it came to getting inside.

But that left the question, what to try now? Since the start, he had been telling himself that he would wait until he actually got to that bridge. And now, there he was, looking over a gaping chasm. Stalling had lost its lustre as an option. He was just going to have to think outside of the box. Assuming that people still worked within its walls, then there had to be some sort of entrance. In all of his time working there, he could not recall a single back entrance. Everyone and everything went through the front doors, with no exceptions. Even the garbage went out through the front. Could one just up and install a new door in the side of such a building? Desmond was a researcher-turned-convict, not an architect or indeed anyone involved in the construction industry. His cousin Dave was a foreman, but that wasn't going to do him much good in the present.

And then, he noticed something, as he stood and pondered, picking the smaller flakes of mud off his trousers. Those front doors… Something was different about them. He took a closer look, believing that perhaps his memory was still acting up. And all the while that he did this, a question burned in his mind:

Why have a padlock for a card-operated door that had long since had its scanner removed?

These doors were different. Aside from the fact that they had none of the collected dust and grime that one would expect considering the rest of the building's surroundings was present, they weren't the automatic doors that BLACKMATTER had installed in place of the old ones back in '90. These were just regular doors, with blacked out windows. He reached out and took hold of the pull handle. They didn't budge. So the padlock must have been keeping them in place. Maybe employees coming and going all had their own keys. And if that was to be the case…

"Shit it all." Desmond grunted as he resisted the urge to launch a kick at the doors. *This* was their entrance. They weren't using any special tricks. In that regard, he was right back to square one, without any immediate way of getting that door opened.

If anything could be called frustrating, that was it. Now what was there?

Nothing. Nothing that he could see. Had he not come far enough? Was God just in a bad mood?

It just… The pure frustration summoned within Desmond an urge that he had not experienced in many a year. The urge to break something, to hurt something. He just wanted to lash out all of his grief and rage on something hard and solid that wouldn't fight back.

And that was just what he did, as he rammed his foot into the bottom end of the dumpster time and time again, inflicting everything that was swelling up inside of him into these clumsily-aimed strikes. It was messy, it was pathetic and he recognised this much within his mind, somewhere buried deep beneath the bursts of passionate anger. But he couldn't stop. It had been so long since he had an outlet, any kind of outlet, for his emotions.

And just like that, it was gone. The rage evaporated, puddles on a warm day. He felt less angry and more embarrassed, an old man striking out at the world around him. And so, he drew to a close and fell still. He didn't exactly feel any better for it, just empty. With a dim sigh, he ran both hands through his hair, angling his head upwards.

His eyes darted over the wall he stood next to, over the filthy smooth nothingness, broken up only by the ventilation cover mounted ever so slightly above the dumpster. He didn't pay attention to it much, not at first. But then, it hit him.

"No." He stated aloud. The idea that flashed in his mind for just a few seconds at the sight was absurd, unthinkable. Absolutely ridiculous.

But then again…

He still wasn't quite sure if he was entirely conscious of what he was doing as he pulled himself up onto that dumpster, balancing on the brittle plastic lid and brought his hands to the grate. Sure enough, a sharp tug brought it away in an instant, affording Desmond a view into the depths of the shaft beyond. It certainly appeared large enough for somebody to fit through, larger than the hole under the fence at least. Even still, this was absurd even by his standards. Was he truly about to do this?

"Brosnan, eat your heart out..." He muttered grimly as he started to haul his body up.

Within the shaft, it was dark. Dark and tight. While not quite as claustrophobic as the fence, he still got the impression of himself as a rat in a maze as he slowly and gratuitously pulled his body weight through, his hair dragging across the top as his shoulders flattened nearly perfectly against the walls. The smell was indescribable, not quite disgusting, but far from what any reasonable person would call pleasant. He was beginning to wish that he had some sort of lighter with him, having any way at all of seeing more than a few inches ahead of his nose, with only the crumpling of metal beneath him to keep him company as he moved forwards into the complete unknown. It only started to occur to him after a few minutes that if he were to make no progress and hit a dead end, then turning back would be a nigh impossibility; He would most likely be left to starve.

He needed to get a grip on his imagination, he told himself, trying to banish such thoughts from his mind. Thinking about that was not likely to help anybody at all, least of all him. He did all he could to keep his mind sharp as he focused on moving and not much else.

Soon, it was to pay off, as he felt a gap beneath his hand. On closer inspection, he realised that he had come across a grate on the bottom of the shaft. A grate that, although it was hard to see through the darkness, appeared to lead down into the building proper. He lowered himself even further and squinted, trying to make out anything beyond the slits of the grate, to little success. He pushed down on it. It rattled stubbornly, not quite ready to come loose just yet. Perhaps with just a bit more force...

Slowly and meticulously, Desmond brought up his leg, twisting it past his torso as he planted it down on the grate, trying his utmost to ignore the pain that jolted through his system, presumably from pulling a muscle, no big surprise with all of this contortionist nonsense. Regardless, he pressed down. Once, then twice, then three times, each with increasing force behind it, doing the best that he could to actually kick the thing in the cramped conditions.

After the fourth kick, he succeeded. The grate burst loose and dropped to the ground below with a resounding clang of metal on tiles. It was a miracle that Desmond himself hadn't gone spiralling down with it, as he remained in the shaft, peering down and feeling oh so thankful to have a taste of something that partially resembled fresh air.

From there, all it took was to drop down himself and this he did without hesitation. It was a longer fall than he had anticipated, but he managed to stick the landing, hitting the ground on his feet with surprising grace. Brushing some loose strands of hair out of his eyes, he glanced up.

It was still dark, although to a far lesser extent than the shaft, and he could make out most of the furniture inhabiting the room. Office cubicles. Yes, he remembered this. This was where most of the above-ground operations were carried out. It seemed to be totally deserted.

His heart was buzzing. He felt an odd combination of nostalgia and terror to be within this room once again, but he couldn't let this override him, not yet. He still had a job to do. He wasn't sure how much he could get out of the sections of the facility that were above the surface, but it was as good a place to start as any.

There was something very eerie about the entire scenario. He had always recalled this room for the life, with lights on and the humming of both employees and their computers as they slaved away, a sense of common comradery that came with all being trapped in a dreadfully dull situation, all of it laid to rust without due cause or even the faintest spark of life within. The only sounds came from the pressing of his soles on the floor. Was this how burglars felt, he wondered.

He entered one of the small cubicles. They were exactly as compact as he remembered, with just enough room for a desk and chair. On the desk, rested a heavy monitor that looked a thousand years detached from what Desmond had seen in that store. He rested his hand on the keyboard; It was positively caked in dust. Was this place simply not being used anymore? The fact that the doors were changed surely confirmed that the facility itself was still in use, but would all be contained within the subterranean levels?

Bending down under the desk, Desmond felt for the PC tower and, once he found it, started to fumble for the power button. Thankfully, his memory served him correct and even in the dark, he managed to find it. With a heavy press, he pushed down on it, coating his finger in a good few inches of dust.

A moment passed. Nothing. He didn't hear that familiar roaring of the system's internals. Much like the office space itself, it appeared devoid of any life. He thumped the case with his fist. Not a peep. Dammit. That wasn't going to work, clearly.

All he could think of was that it either wasn't plugged into the wall or this part of the building simply didn't have any power. Both were equally likely. Investigating further, Desmond got down onto his knees and pushed his head underneath the desk. He had to hold back the urge to choke violently on the dust down there. In the darkness, he grasped around for the power socket. When he eventually found it, he got a handful of nothing. There was certainly no lead plugged in. In fact, he couldn't locate a lead anywhere.

This would be a hell of a lot easier if he had a torch, he swore to God...

Before he could ramble internally for any longer period of time, he was alerted by the suddenness of unanticipated footsteps. The creaking of an opening door accompanying them, they carried throughout the room.

As the realisation seeped in, Desmond's heart skipped a beat and he nearly shot right up, narrowly avoiding slamming his head on the underside of the desk. No lights turned on and no voices could be heard, just the dull, melodic patter of heavy boots that didn't appear to have any rhyme, reason or intended destination. Just... Pacing.

Almost subconsciously, Desmond pulled the rest of his body under the desk, concealing himself in the shadows to the very best of his abilities, elbows pressed into the tower. He fought back a bitter laugh as, in spite of the situation, he wondered just how many times he was going to end up in cramped spaces today. All the while, the steps persevered.

From where he lay curled, he caught sight of a beam of light, a thin white strip that illuminated the room's swirling particles as it cut through the blackness. A flashlight, most likely. Security? Briefly, Desmond's mind flashed to old Bobby Carter, the facility's primary security officer back in the day. It seemed rather unlikely that it was still the same man in charge, but he couldn't help but think what would happen if it was him. He imagined it wouldn't be all friendly.

...

He groaned softly. What the hell was he doing? At a time like this, the absolute last thing that he needed was for his mind to flirt with any ideas other than the most immediate.

The beam drew all the closer, uncaring for the circumstances of Desmond's mind; And then, it shone in all of its radiance.

The owner of the flashlight stepped into the cubicle.

Five

His breath was left ragged as if it had followed an encounter with a jet turbine, and yet he could not say a word, could not make a single sound. This patroller, whoever they may have been, was now firmly within the cubicle, even as Desmond could see only dark polished boots from where he lay. With careful subtlety, he brought his good hand up to his mouth as he felt his pupils shrink within their sockets. The fear paralysed him, leaving him unable - even if he was willing - to make the slightest movement aside from the gentle vibrations as he shook and watched those boots. It was as if he was a child, hiding from his father's wrath.

The beam of the flashlight spilled onto the floor, painting it in a visible glow that revealed the flooring to Desmond for the first time, tiled and certainly less than well-maintained. Cracks and grime spread out, forming demented patterns of inconceivable meaning and all that he could do was stare.

The beam began to move, gradually and with utter precision, swaying across the floor and coming to the desk. He pushed himself back as far as he could, fighting to remain out of the light, no easy feat considering that he had to simultaneously ensure he made not the slightest noise. How much stress could one person take? Being in prison was a hell of a lot better than this. Even if he was always looking over his shoulder, at least he had free range of movement.

A moment passed, as did the flashlight's beam, trailing up to the top of the desk, apparently having missed Desmond entirely, through some miracle of nature. He knew he couldn't relax yet, but he felt the small spikes of dopamine in his brain as it vanished and he was left staring at those dark boots again.

Without warning, the boot rushed to meet him.

There was no time to even curse out in anxiety as the cap struck Desmond in the chin, snapping his head back as the pain swarmed in unbearable clusters. He bit down on his own tongue and very nearly screamed, as he was grabbed by the tie and pulled out violently from under the desk.

It was him. The man in black from the previous day. That much was evident even in the darkness, as he stared down at a struggling Desmond with no discernable emotion. His grip was most comparable to a vice, unrelenting as it dragged the former inmate up to his feet, all the while blood dribbled from the corners of his mouth.

"You were asked to be smart." The man sighed as he pressed Desmond's back to the cubicle wall. "Was it so hard to manage that?"

He had no answer. His mind was cracking open with a thousand panicked thoughts, feeling the intensity of the man's stare even behind the dark glasses. Limply, he raised an arm to launch a flailing strike at his captor's head, but he clearly saw it coming and grabbed the arm with his remaining hand, twisting it all the way around and threatening to snap it in two. The pain that resulted could only be equated to the blow to his hand that he had received all of those years ago.

"Damn…" He grunted, unable to hold back his vocal chords, before he was brought closer to the man and then slammed back into the wall again. There, he was dropped, where he folded like a deck chair. The back of his head throbbed, pulsing gingerly as he struggled to look up at his assailant. Doing so sank his heart faster than anything else in the world.

"You should have made yourself scarce." The man sighed as he pointed the revolver, meral glistening in the darkness, directly at Desmond's forehead. "No more second chances."

Fight or flight kicked in instantly, and Desmond lunged forwards, grabbing for the gun and throwing it off his own face as the trigger was pulled. The bang echoed through his ears as the room was momentarily lit up by the revolver's flash, the bullet tearing through the wall behind him. With the precious few femtoseconds of distraction, he burst away from the cubicle, even while the gun was pointed at him once again. He didn't even think, he just ran, bolting past the series of cubicles that lined the sides of the room, his entire body pumping with adrenaline.

In those crucial moments, he acted frantically, a caged animal, turning where he lay and swiping at his attacker, managing to feebly grab the gun, trying his best to force it away from his own head. For his efforts, he received a blow to the ribcage, a blow too devastating to come from any normal human surely, but he held on, gritting his teeth and biting down on his lip.

All of a sudden, the man almost appeared to relinquish control of the gun, Desmond bringing it away in his own hands as he stumbled back. Now holding it, and putting at much distance between himself and his now-unmoving attacker, he examined it. A heavy, ugly instrument of death. Just looking at it reminded him of his sins. Flashing before his eyes, he saw the blood spurting from her stomach, the look of utter hatred, and just a hint of wounded betrayal, that had been in her eyes. The bile rose up in his throat, his eyes shook.

And then, he raised the gun and he fired, directly into his assailant's chest.

As the bullet made impact, the man stumbled, struggling to stay upright. With a newfound resolve, a desire to put him into the ground, Desmond fired three more times, hitting his stomach and left shoulder. He made no noise as he brought his gloved hand to the first wound, all while Desmond retained their distance, firearm still pointed.

Then, he looked up, unfazed. Not Desmond. The man.

"What the hell..." He muttered to himself; He had to be seeing things. As the man straightening his body up again, he looked for all the world as if he had not experienced even the slightest hint of pain. Thrown off for only a second, and his terror delving into hew layers, Desmond squeezed the trigger.

A dull click sounded out.

Empty.

The two men stared at one another, one a portrait of horror, the other as calm as a swallow. Then, Desmond tossed the gun aside and he ran. He didn't think, he couldn't think; He just sprinted.

Finding the door, he thrust forth his elbow and bashed it open, coming out into the facility's main reception lobby, which was as seemingly abandoned as the rest of the place. Scanning the room, he took note of the two elevators mounted alongside each other on the far wall and adjacent to those, the set of doors that led outside, open by a crack with faint light streaming through.

He had no clue how much time he had, but he knew that it wasn't much. He had a choice: Take the elevator, the leftmost elevator, one that he had taken most everyday for years, and continue what he had come here for, or cut his losses right then and there and come back at a later date. The latter was absurd, unthinkable in every possible measure. Now that the mystery stalker-come-attempted assassin of his knew that he wasn't going to play ball, he couldn't take a step without having to look over his shoulder. If he went back to that awful motel room now, there would be no guarantee of a next day.

He ran to the lift. Doors were bolted shut without hint of any way to open them. To their left, a scanner. Now, that was a new addition. Desmond resisted the urge to punch the damned thing as he stared at it. All of that and he was back needing the key card again. This time, there wasn't any trick to pull to get himself to his destination; This elevator was the only way down to the facility's lower levels, that was a basic fact that could not be subverted. Now, what the hell was he meant to do?

He heard the door from behind him opening and he had not a second to react, although that was all that he needed. He made a break for the exit, pumping his arms as he sprinted faster than he ever recalled doing in the past. "Dammit..." He grunted to himself, not even taking another look into the facility as he burst through the doors, coming back out into the hazy early afternoon atmosphere, thick with smog and the greys of the skies above.

That was one problem partially solved, feeling the relatively fresh air filling his lungs and providing a temporary relief. But although in the protection of the outside, he was still very much within the compound, and he somewhat doubted that he would be able to crawl back under that fence again before he was caught up to by his stalker.

But that was hardly something that was in any position to halt him for the moment and so, he ran blindly. If he couldn't go under, then he was just going to have to risk it with that barbed wire on top. For the time being, cutting himself to ribbons was preferable to death. Marginally.

He leapt at that fence with an unquellable ferocity, slotting the fingers of his good hand between the wires, and began to scale. He had done a bit of rock climbing in his youth, but back then, he had the luxury of two hands, not to mention the fact that a cliff face usually didn't bend and sway in the breeze with all of the structural stability of a paper cup in a thunderstorm. His right arm hung pointlessly as he scrambled, forcing his shoes through the gaps that were just a little too small, in order to get a foothold. This was a day of perhaps his least dignified moments, but that hardly bothered him at a time like this.

Within moments, he had managed to reach the top and there he was, eye level with the tangled, angry strips of barbed wire, waiting eagerly to slice him the instant that he drew near. He thought quickly and shook his arm a little, retracting his hand inside of his sleeve and bunching it up against the fabric. From there, he gently took hold of the wire and lifted himself up and over it. This was by no means a master plan, he barely had the strength to support his trembling form with one hand as he hauled, but with no other options at hand, it was his best bet for the time being.

Just like that, he was up. And in as sudden a flourish, he was over, sailing above the enraged strands of coiling dark wire and gripping the fence on the other side for an easy descent. That was the basic idea, at least; It proved slightly less effective as Desmond missed the grasp and plummeted straight down to the mud below.

He hit the ground at an odd angle, felt his arm bend in ways that it definitely was not supposed to. Dammit. His little feat of physical strength there had blinded him to the basic fact that he was still an ever-ageing man with a bad hand. It took a few moments, seeped in both light pain and a sense of humiliation, to pull himself back up, where he brushed off the worst of the mud. Thank God for a coat, and the fact that his suit was relatively cheap.

Straightening up, he looked over his shoulder and through that cross hatched fence, he saw his stalker, the man in black. He simply stood there, unmoving and seemingly unemotional. Watching, eyes behind those black lenses that permitted no sight of what lay behind.

Desmond bit back his tongue, resisting the urge to say anything to the man as he stood his ground for just a moment longer, then he turned and ran. Getting out of there as soon as possible, putting as much distance between himself and the man, that was all that he needed.

Run, run and keep running. That was his present mantra, and he followed it to a T, his strained legs carrying his body as far from that facility as they possibly could. He was no Sebastian Cole, but he gave it his all, right as he burst away from the swampy grasslands, came around a corner and fell right into the path of an oncoming car.

All at once, the noise lit up his ears. The blaring of a horn, the scurry of startled wildlife and the dim clang of metal as it hit him and sent him reeling back, unharmed for the most part, but dazed.

For a while, he simply lay there, his vision clouding over with dark rims, his eyes heavy, his entire body u willing to move. He could hear panicked conversation in the background, but it was too faint in his ringing ears to make sense of what exactly it was. He layand he focused on his breathing, even as out of his peripheral vision, a young woman wheeled herself over to where he lay.

"Oh God…" She gasped as she brought her hand over her mouth. "I… Roger, I think I know this guy…"

Six

Everything that came next felt like a bizarre fever dream, one that Desmond hung in stilted obliviousness of, unable to get a read on what was going on. He did not resist as the woman fawned over him, nor as her accomplice, a rather tall, well-groomed looking man, helped him to his feet, and as he sat in the back of that car, headed to God knows where, he didn't say a word. He was drifting in and out of consciousness, the scenery through the windows mixing with his imagination to create indecipherable images. Every so often, he picked up on a word or two between the pair in the front seats.

"Has this town even got a hospital?" The more masculine of the couple enquired, sounding rather exhausted for the most part.

"There was a clinic." The woman reasoned. "Dunno if it's still there. You said yourself that it doesn't look too serious, right?"

The man's voice raised just a little in volume. "Well, yeah, but we're not seriously gonna bring this random guy around with us..."

"He's not random." She exclaimed, exasperated. "If it's who I think it is…" She then fell silent as she looked over her shoulder into the back; All Desmond could see was a dark silhouette, the light catching on the ends of her hairs and the rims of her glasses.

"And if it isn't?"

Desmond didn't hear much more of the discussion, his grip on the land of the living fading. His mind was growing dull, his adrenaline had died out. The shapes that he saw before his eyes were growing less and less recognisable, his lids getting heavier to maintain. He was exhausted.

When he could keep his eyes open no longer, he closed them for just a moment; Opening them, he was in an entirely different scene.

They were gathered around a lunch table, all of them. Desmond, Simon, Paul, Lucy. The room was bright and well lit and awash with life and vibrancy, so far removed from the cool darkness of the car mere moments ago. It was pleasant, it was nostalgic. They were discussing something; Desmond couldn't quite recall what the conversation's start point was.

"You're mad." Lucy sighed with a roll of her eyes. "You really think Liotta would make a gangster?"

"I'm telling you," Simon protested. "I saw the film last night, it was good."

"I can't see it." Lucy shook her head. "Ray Liotta." She repeated. "Not a chance would he do a good mobster."

"It could be worth a shot." A younger, more well-cut and somewhat more handsome Desmond spoke up from where he sat, picking at his pasta with a plastic spork. "Maybe he can play a good bad guy, you won't know until you see it. I'll give it a go, at least."

"Yeah, go right ahead." Simon sighed. "Don't knock it 'til you've tried it, like Des said."

At that point, Desmond looked up from his food. "What do you reckon, Paul?"

As a response to this, Stanton grunted disapprovingly. Clearly, they were not going to be getting much out of him.

Needless to say, the conversation fell to an end as the presence of Doctor Acker was suddenly made clear. Looking up at her, her face was a mess of distorted flashes, indecipherable, and she spoke in a low husky tone that was most definitely inaccurate to her actual voice.

"Doc," Simon nodded. "All good?"

"Mhm. And yourself?" Doctor Acker always had been like this; Not quite as aloof as Paul, but very close to it.

"I mean, sure, I'm good. Good as I could be, probably." He let out a low sigh, suggesting that he was already exhausted of having to talk to his superior; Sensing his friend's pain, Desmond had taken over.

"How's Penny, then?" He asked curiously, tilting his head to the side in a manner that looked a hint like an inquisitive puppy.

Acker adjusted her glasses. "She's fine. Giving off about school again."

"Aye, what kid isn't?" Simon point out in jest, providing a little shrug of his attitude. "You show me any kid who ever wanted to be there and I'll show you the case to bring back lobotomies."

"Classy…" Lucy groaned after a shared exasperated stare with Desmond. "I'm glad to hear you've got an endless wealth of empathy for your fellow man."

To this, Simon glanced back with a coy grin. "They're children, not people."

This was it. This was what Desmond had missed, without even realising it, and in these moments, he was offered a window into that old life, a life that was completely normal, without murder, without conspiracy and without any problems beyond trying to get the day's work down. Such a peaceful existence. So very enviable…

…

And just like that, it was gone. He had grasped it for a few moments and then it was offered to him for no longer. Reality settled back in and the stark whites gave way to a cooler, darker environment. Wherever he was now lying, it was not doing wonders for his back and as he looked around, craning his neck painfully, the most he could tell himself was that, at the very least, it was better than the motel that he was used to. Cleaner, bigger and appearing to stretch on beyond one room, as evidenced by the multiple doors dotted around the walls. This room in question looked to be some form of living-come-dining room, a row of culinary appliances transitioning into a small television and coffee table opposing the sofa that he found himself to be lying on, an old and ragged yet well loved blanket resting across his knees.

He was readying his attempts to pull his body up into a sitting position when his attention was grabbed by the clattering of wheels against a wooden flooring. The lights came on and there at the far end of the room, sat the same young woman from the car. Her hazel eyes were encased behind thin spectacles, her auburn hair short and somewhat wild. Desmond knew this woman. He knew her well.

"Mister Ford…" She mumbled softly as she slowly wheeled herself nearer to where he lay. "It is you, right?"

"Yeah." Again hauling himself up, he placed both feet on the cold yet comfortable floor and rested his forehead in one hand. "The one and only…"

"So, you're out of prison, then?" She questioned tentatively. "I didn't think it would be so…"

"Soon?" He found the word for her. "Neither could I. Assuming that I pay attention to the terms of parole, though, that's how things have turned out." Thinking about it, he had to imagine that his recent escapades had to be some sort of violation of those terms. Not that it was even close to his biggest concern right now. "Why-"

His question was interrupted as a new man entered the room, that well-built fellow from earlier. His eyes darted around, first from Desmond and then to the woman. "He good, Al?"

"He seems fine, thank you." She nodded as she grasped the rim of her glasses. "He's conscious now, at least."

"Al?" Desmond asked, glancing at her.

"Alice." She quickly returned.

"Oh, right then…"

Regardless of Desmond's thoughts on the matter, he was cut short as the other man approached him.

"Roger Baxter." He introduced himself with a dry grin as he went to shake Desmond's hand. "You gave us quite a scare there, Sir."

"Thanks…" He accepted the shake. "Desmond Ford."

All at once, Roger's stare hardened and that grip grew just a hint tighter. The room became just a bit colder. "Ford." Clearly, he knew the name.

"Mhm hm." Desmond confirmed; He saw no reason not to at this point.

"The convict?"

"Ex-convict, but that's the one, yes."

Roger looked over his shoulder. Back to Desmond. Then to the door. Then, another cursory glance around the entire room. "Get the hell out."

"Roger!" Alice practically exploded, as she wheeled herself closer to the two. "It's alright, okay?"

"Alright, is it?" He scoffed. "Alright having a con in our place? A Goddamn murderer at that?"

Desmond resisted the urge to make some sort of bleak quip about the situation as he pulled himself to his feet, almost instantly stumbling with his legs barely able to support him. "Perhaps I should leave." He appreciated the hospitality, but it wasn't as if he had no reason to get right back to the prowl as soon as was possible. All of this was just a surprise distraction, one that he doubted he had much time for.

"Wait, wait!" Called Alice. "If we just calm down a second-"

"Door's thataway." Roger tilted his head in the direction of the exit, completely blindsiding his wife's words.

"Thanks." As he tried to walk to the door, he became acutely aware of just how much of a hobble he had been reduced to. His legs really were not in a good mood, not that he could blame them, considering the events of the past...

He stopped in his tracks. "How long has it been, if I can ask?"

"Four hours, give or take." The cross-armed man answered instantly.

"Four hours." Desmond repeated with a desert's throat, nodding. "Thank you."

And just like that, he was out of the door, out of the Baxters' residence and onto the front porch. From the looks of things, it was some sort of holiday BnB; The development must have been fairly new, for he recognised absolutely none of this from his past. It was definitely still Greenrock, though. It retained that vibe. Only the gods could possibly know why someone would want to spend a holiday there or all towns, but the world was full of surprises.

He limped down across the front lawn, which was surprisingly well-tamed, all things considered. When he was about halfway there, a voice halted him.

"Mister Ford?"

He looked over his shoulder. There, Alice sat, hands resting on the wheels of her chair as she lingered in the doorway.

"I'm sorry about that." She professed, rolling her eyes behind those steel spectacles. "Roger's… Well…"

"Roger's totally justified." Desmond shrugged. "Can't say I would react differently were I in his position. A convict in his home probably isn't the best way to kick off a holiday."

"Probably not…" Alice mused. "Still… Are you staying in Greenrock right now?"

Desmond's mind flashed to that dilapidated motel. "For all intents and purposes. I've got that business to take care of."

"Ah. That business." From the woman's tone, it was clear that she had very much expected it to be behind them forever; Perhaps she had thought he would have forgotten over the decades. No such luck. "Well… Roger and I are here for the memorial. It's nearly that time, you know."

"Ah." Desmond gently moved his hands to his coat pockets. "They have one?"

"It's official, per se, but…" She shrugged. "I like to come down to pay my respects each year."

After a moment where the two simply stared at one another from across the grass, Desmond nodded. "Fair enough. Maybe I'll see you around then."

"Yeah…" Alice glanced down, like she was about to say something, but then decided against it and kept her mouth shut. With one final nod in her direction, he began to walk away once again.

Once mode, he heard her voice; This time, he did not turn. "O'Connor wasn't… He never was in his right mind, was he?"

He managed to walk a few more paces before stopping short. His whole body felt as if it had seized up for a moment. He dipped his head, shadowing his face, as he fought to keep his mouth from breaking into a frown.

"O'Connor…" He finally said, voice low and regretful and a little raspy. "We used him. We're the reason why he did what he did."

He said no more. He couldn't say anymore. He left the property and kept walking through the early dusk, the oranges beaming down on him and basking him in a faintly warm glow that did little to distract from the cold seeping from both the atmosphere and from within Desmond. Eventually, he came to a bus stop, and there he waited.

It took twenty minutes for a bus to arrive and another thirty for one that would take him near his actual desired destination. Desmond was surprised that he was even that lucky, for he never had really trusted public transport at the best of times, least of all in a place as desolate as Greenrock. The bus was, somewhat less surprisingly, almost empty, allowing him a seat by himself close to the back. His seat was far from clean, but considering his current state, he was not about to be picky. He needed a shower and a proper rest.

The journey back was a slow one, the bus moving at a speed that was not exactly set to wow anybody, and so it allowed Desmond the time to simply think about everything, primarily the last few hours.

It was only at this point when the fact of what he had seen at the facility struck him. The adrenaline had finally calmed down somewhat and he realised that his stalker... He had shrugged off those bullets like they were nothing. It had to have been a trick of the light, or perhaps of Desmond's own mind. There hadn't been any blood, any sign of pain, just a couple of holes in that immaculate dark suit and a brief pause for recovery. There was something... Deeply inhuman about it all. Something that could not be so easily dismissed.

This man knew where he was. That much was obvious. For all that he knew, he would be arriving back at the motel to find the stalker waiting for him, and that would be the end of that. Desmond was fairly certain that he was beginning to run out of lucky escapes. Whoever that man was, he surely now knew that idle threats would not work. Escalation was the logical conclusion. It was only just dawning on him that returning to his room may be a non-option.

"Damn…"

It wouldn't have mattered much to him, except that he had his money and spare clothes in there, two things he desperately needed. He started to wrack his brain, only slightly thrown off as the bus lurched over a speed bump with a groaning of creaking metal and nearly flung him directly off his seat.

Perhaps it was not the most solid idea in the world, but he could always, he reckoned, take to reception, ask that girl at the desk if she had seen anyone who wasn't a regular patron head in the direction of his room. One, after all, had to pass through to get to where the main rooms were located. If not, perhaps he could risk it. He was fairly certain that, at the very least, no issues would arise from that, surely.

He made up his mind and moved on from the subject before he had time to second-guess himself. Alice - as she was now going by - was back. He couldn't help but chuckle grimly at the coincidence of her being the one to come across him. Without her and Roger, he would likely already be dead. Perhaps he would send a gift basket if he came out of the other end of this alive. Even still, her return reminded him of something greater. The anniversary, seventeen years since it all went so awfully wrong, and their lives were all changed irreparably.

Andrew O'Connor... The man had been a hero, abandoned by the government he had served. And they - BLACKMATTER and Acker and Desmond himself - had toyed with him. Made him a guinea pig. And it had all gone so terribly awry. Icarus had lived up to its namesake. Six people dead. With a bit of luck, if there was a Heaven, O'Connor was now up there. He had not deserved any of it.

The bus eventually came to a halt at a stop a few blocks away from the motel and Desmond departed, pausing in the gangway to allow an elderly woman, skin pulled tight like a hotel sheet, to pass by him. He was grateful for the walk, for his legs felt as if they could give out at any point and were certainly overdue some stretching. He couldn't relax, though; Not yet.

It was with growing apprehension that he approached the motel, almost creeping at points, although it was with some relief that he saw there to be no black cars in the parking lot. A few old beaten sedans and a white Dodge Charger bearing the red lights and livery of the Greenrock Sheriff's Department. Considering the state of the place, he assumed they were settling some domestic dispute.

Regardless, he entered the reception, having to pull a little on the stuck door. Inside, the place was empty, save for the receptionist herself and what looked to be two officers. As Desmond approached, the girl looked up, eyes widening, and pointed to him. Odd.

Odder still was when the officers turned to face him.

"Can I help you?" Desmond asked, hoping not to appear as too suspicious after his evening, noting the pair to be the sheriff and a deputy. "From the way you're looking at me, I'm guessing you want something."

He already knew this was coming, but it still hit him harder than any bullet as he heard it.

"Desmond Ford?" The sheriff asked in a low drawl.

"That's me, yes." This was definitely not going to end well.

"Right." He seemed almost apologetic. "Look, fella, we're gonna need to have a few words with you, alright? We've gotten some reports. About an unregistered firearm in your possession."

Seven

Overall, they were rather pleasant to him. At first.

That died down somewhat after he asserted that he had no clue what they were talking about for the fifteenth time.

There he sat, his hands bound together by the heavy chains that he had not expected to be wearing again so soon, in a little concrete room without windows, without any furniture save for the flimsy table that a little paper cup of water rested upon.

"I just- I don't know what I'm supposed to say." He sighed as he brought his chained hands up to his head, brushing some hair out of his eyes. "I haven't had any contact with any firearms since I was released, nor any point before that, for that matter."

The sheriff was obviously getting agitated, tapping his fingers on the table as he sat sideways on his own seat, eyes narrowed to little black dots.

"And I'll keep telling you 'til the cows come home that we found the firearm in question in your little motel room. No serial number, covered in your fingerprints and fired recently, might I add." The frustration in his voice was palpable, each word threatening to spill over into vicious rage. "What, you gonna tell us that you've got some döppleganger out there, framing you for it." An angry chuckle followed. "This shit ain't just gonna go away, Ford. Let's put aside the matter of it being unlicensed. You're on parole. We have your file."

"Seventeen years for murder." The young deputy added from where he stood by the door, the only escape from the tight, lifeless room. "A violation like this'll see you another couple, at least."

Desmond sighed into his arms. He was still exhausted from the previous evening, he was barely able to process the information flung at him, let alone comprehend the severity of the situation. Everything seemed so massive right now. Too massive. His head hurt.

"All I can keep saying…" He muttered. "... Is that I haven't been near any gun, licensed or otherwise."

Was that true? He couldn't even remember. He certainly hadn't kept one in the motel room, if nothing else. Alas, nothing he could say was going to explain this away easily. He was starting to realise that much. He was in a tight situation, and wriggling out of it was surely due to be an impossibility, even if it weren't for the sheriff's visibly escalating irritation.

But still, he gave him nothing, and they repaid that favour. When it became entirely clear that they would not be getting anywhere for the time being, the interview came to an end. Desmond found himself being heaved by the shoulders down the short, narrow corridor and the process began. His suit was abandoned, returned to the all-too familiar county blues, and he was given a cell, a thin, concrete room with enough space to manoeuvre, more or less, and a slim hatch on the door that allowed him to look out into the lifeless hall beyond. In prison, he had been used to howling and screaming and banging from his neighbours; Here, it was deathly quiet. He had no neighbours. It was just him.

For a while, he paced, feeling the glorified potato sack hang from his narrow frame. When his legs grew tired and his mind grew too dim to ruminate, he sat on the provided mattress.

What now?

That was the question of the year.

The more that he thought about it, the more he understood the gravity of where he was. A violent offender, a murderer, caught with a parole violation as severe as an unregistered firearm. He would be lucky if he didn't die before his sentence ended. And what could he do? They had the gun and they had his prints on it. The matter did not get much simpler than that. Of course, it was not his own welfare that bothered him. What panged at his heart in short, sharp shreds of guilt, was the knowledge that he would be unable to fulfil his mission from behind bars. He was right back at square one with nothing to show for it but the brunt of BLACKMATTER's ire.

Sleep did not come easily, but when it eventually did, it was about as peaceful as one could expect. Imagery whipped past his vision faster than he could register it, bursts of static accompanied with low, animal howls, shattering glass.

He could make out some of the images but just barely. He saw the dusty television screen and the footage broadcast upon it with a low hum of the lights behind it. He saw the view of the helicopter's camera, recording the events down below, on the steps of the church. He saw O'Connor, staring down the police while shouldering his rifle. He saw him, as he had seen all those years ago, bring the rifle up to his chin and splatter his brains over the steps behind him. All the while, the screaming and the crackling continued.

Just like that, he was in the laboratory, deep below the surface. The terrified wailings of Penny pierced his ears. He saw the body, blood gushing from the wound in the chest of the woman who stood just opposite him, her face cloaked in violent, angry shadow. The blood was gushing out at an inhuman pace, more than any person would have in their body. He felt as sick as he had when it had first happened.

And then, the noise cleared and, with total silence settling in, he heard her final word again, echoing in his ears, the word that had accompanied her cold body hitting the floor.

"Penelope…"

And then, it all faded, and Desmond was awake again, lying at an awkward angle on the mattress with the sweat coating his skin. He did not sleep again that night. He merely lay and he thought hollow, dry thoughts.

That same day, only a few hours later, he received a visitor. All that the sheriff told him as he marched him to the meeting room was that it was his attorney. Desmond's curiosity was only somewhat piqued by this, for his previous attorney, one Ray Sheen, was both a public defender with no real reason to come back to his client and, as far as Desmond could recall, currently in prison himself for perjury. He had figured that he would probably get assigned another PD, assuming that it even got that far, and he doubted they would have any interest in visiting him until he was at least in a more permanent facility.

Entering the blank room, he was greeted with a rather unremarkable-looking fellow, a short, weasley gentleman with thick glasses and a slate grey combover that was almost certainly a toupé. He looked too small for his suit and his face was mostly nose. Utterly unremarkable but, surprisingly to Desmond, oddly familiar. Not in a personal sense, of course, more in the sense of someone whom he had seen in the papers at some point.

Cautiously, he ventured further into the room and took a seat on the other side of the table from the gentleman. The sheriff nodded and left the room, shutting the door behind him. Only then, did the man speak.

"Desmond Ford." He started in a nasally tone. "I'm Gerry Price. I'm an attorney."

"Price…" Desmond muttered to himself. It sounded very faintly recognisable. And then, it hit him. "The celebrity lawyer?"

Price gave a moorish little grin that only furthered the comparisons to a nervous mole rat. "The one and only. And, as of 2006, the primary attorney for BLACKMATTER Incorporated."

Ah. Now, it was beginning to make sense. Desmond practically felt himself shrivelling in his chair.

Price lifted up his leather briefcase and set it on the table. "As a former employee, BLACKMATTER are very kindly offering my services to you."

"They're not, are they?" Desmond was in no mood for any of this nonsense; If they could get to the point as soon as possible, then that would be just fine by him.

Price faltered. "Well... Anyway, you seem to be in quite a bit of trouble here."

"Surprisingly enough, Gerry, I'm not a child, I can see that rather clearly."

The poor man looked like he was about to drop unconscious right there and then. "Oh! R-right, then! We'll... We'll get to business then." He clipped open his case and drew out a hefty file. "BLACKMATTER wanted me to inform you that, uh, if you face down this conviction quietly and return to incarceration without raising any trouble,then you shall face no further repercussions."

Desmond tapped the table impatiently. "You mean that I won't be killed, don't you?"

Despite everything, there was something vaguely satisfying about seeing the sweat that clung to Price's face like a second skin. "Well, I, uh, would never confirm such a thing. I'm… Sure you're overreacting."

"Sure." Desmond leaned back in his seat. He was getting a strong read on this guy. As weak-willed as they came. He wasn't resilient and he wasn't taking any pleasure in this. He was a useful stooge for BLACKMATTER to make their message clear. And the message was "Stand down and you'll keep your life." What a pathetic bargain. As if his life meant anything anymore.

"So, to move on, they asked me to make it clear in no uncertain terms to you that if you, um, do anything to cause them any further embarrassment, the consequences will be… Dire." His voice broke with that final word, producing a rather amusing shriek from the lawyer.

"In other words, as I said earlier, I'll be killed."

"H-hey! I never said…"

"I can read implications, Gerry. And while you might want to keep your conscience clear of this, there's no reason to sugarcoat it." Desmond leaned back in. "I know the power that BLACKMATTER holds. I can imagine it's even greater than it was back in the day. I don't know who they've got in their pocket, but I'm willing to bet it's a good deal. And do you know what, Gerry?" He put on a sickeningly false gentle tone. "I don't really give a damn. All this power, that they sent a little rat person to sort me out? You hand out these threats as if you're talking to a man who values his life."

He saw Price's entire body tense up gloriously. Desmond knew how childish he was being, but… It felt so good to finally have one of BLACKMATTER's minions who could be bullied even by him. Just a tiny bit of personal karma, for all they had put him through.

As Desmond leaned forwards, Price leaned back, until he was pushing on the back legs of his chair. "Please, this is absurd, Mister Ford, I don't know what you're talking about- M-maybe we could arrange some psychiatric consultations, we could use it in your defence."

"Ah, a bat ward." He mimed a little sarcastic clap. "Well, wouldn't that be so convenient for you? Thanks, but no thanks."

"You're-" And that was when the chair had been pushed to his limits. Price fell back, hitting the ground with a crash. Almost instantly, the sheriff raced back into the room, grabbing at Desmond; He did not resist as he was hauled out of his seat and had his shoulders pinned firmly to his sides.

"You-" Struggling to maintain what little composure he had left, Price tried to pick himself up, his toupé misaligned and his suit disturbed. "You're making a mistake, Ford! You know what, when you're rotting in a cell, I'll be laughing and sipping on my gin!" His voice sharpened; Clearly, he was more able to play the big man now that the sheriff was in there to back him up. "Officer, remove this animal from my sight!"

"I love you too, Gerry." At this point, Desmond just felt like being inflammatory as he was bundled out of the room. "I hope that BLACKMATTER pays you enough to cover that fake tan."

Childish. But he couldn't deny that it helped him feel just a little better about himself, even as he was taken back to that blank little room. It wasn't as if there was a whole lot he could do other than sit or pace, and ruminate.

It seemed that at a certain point, things had just gone… Wrong. Him. He and Simon and Lucy and Paul and Bobby and even Acker to some extent. They had been closer than mere coworkers. They were all in on the same ambitions. They were going to change the world for the better, they were going to give a new chance at life to those who had suffered for too long. All of that altruism, where did it end up going?

Andrew O'Connor had joined them in early 1991, sent to the Greenrock Facility by the BLACKMATTER higher ups. He never really was part of the team. He was more a guinea pig. A veteran, O'Connor had lost his left arm in Iraq. One could only imagine the condition he was in when he agreed to partake in the programme. So, he became Icarus' first official test subject.

It had been going so well. But these things never lasted. October Thirty-First, 1992. That was when it happened. O'Connor snapped. Icarus malfunctioned, it broke his mind. Five people died by his hand before he turned his gun on himself. And that was that. That was when everything fell apart. It was less than twenty-four hours later when Desmond would commit his final atrocity. Paul was smart, he and Bobby and Lucy and even

Simon. They had kept their mouths shut and kept their freedom, as far as he knew. But not Desmond. He couldn't. Just like Stanton said, he had probably gone and made things worse.

What could he have done? Nothing, nothing at all. He knew Acker. He knew that she would have done to Penny exactly what had been done to O'Connor. She was hellbent. After everything, after all of the times he had dropped Penny off at school, after he ate dinner under their roof, he couldn't let it slide.

Ridiculous…

Without even realising it, he found himself with his back to the wall, gently sliding down until he was in a half-sitting, half-crouched position, head pointed up to the featureless ceiling as if he was looking for God himself.

He must have been starting to go truly mad, because as he looked back down, he could swear that he saw Penny, sitting there before him, not ageing a day past '92. She didn't speak. Of course she didn't. She was an illusion, a construct of his exhausted mind, sitting there and staring at him with a face that could not be read.

He recalled the day that he had first heard of Penny. It had been sometime in the late eighties, the group had been discussing their plans for the future, for they were mostly still rather young at that point. There, it had been revealed that Doctor Acker had a daughter. They never really learned what happened to the father, but he certainly was not in the picture by that time. Not long after, Acker formally introduced her to the team during a dinner.

Penny was physically disabled; In spite of such, she was as sweet as could be. Desmond, Simon, Lucy, they had become honorary aunt and uncles to her. Maybe even Paul. To the infertile Desmond, she had become the daughter he never could have. He would have died for her. And in the end, he killed for her.

The memory was raw, more vivid than it had been in years. He killed Acker, as Penny watched. He had taken that knife and plunged it into her, again and again, until she fell. And for what?

Because Acker hadn't learned. Because Acker was willing to repeat the mistakes she had made with O'Connor. For that, the house of cards had fallen. Or so, many would have thought. But with her dying breaths. Desmond had seen the tenacity on display; He had seen how obsessed she was with seeing Icarus through. And he knew that she would not be alone. BLACKMATTER would not pull the plug. Maybe they had no right to. But he couldn't let it continue.

Oversized children playing God. That was what they had been. It was what BLACKMATTER continued to be. It fell on him to bring it all crashing down.

The question was, how was he supposed to do that, from the wrong side of a barred door?

Eight

Two more days passed in that little cell in the sheriff's office, two nigh-agonising days of trying desperately to find some sort of solution to his mess. On the third day, they came for him.

It was the deputy from before who opened the door, that plump, unassuming young fellow who had a distinct lack of experience radiating from him. He stood in the doorway, announced to Desmond that he was being transferred. That meant that the end was present.

He stood from his mattress without question. He had figured that this was coming and was only surprised that it had taken so long. Someone like him, they wouldn't want to keep in a place like this for too long; As soon as the Corrections Department could move him to a proper facility, the better.

"Right, keep your hands in view." The deputy ordered as he waded in, practically reading directly from a cue card. From his belt, he produced the handcuffs, rustling with a metallic clink as he brought them up. "Outstretched."

"Sure." Desmond nodded. "Outstretched." He began to do so. All the while, his mind played through a thousand different thoughts. Once he was out of Greenrock, that would be it. He was done. He would live out to the end of his days in prison and, of far more concern to him, he would never fulfil his mission, his promise.

As his mind rushed through this, he body seemed to act without command. Before he had a chance to restrain himself, his good hand shot forwards, clipped the deputy on the chin. He stumbled, letting out a grunt and a curse, and Desmond charged what body weight he had into him, pushing him back towards the door and ramming his head up, sending his forehead into the deputy's jaw.

Pain cracked through him, but he was too filled with adrenaline to question that now. He was a wild animal, the lion in the colosseum and as the poor deputy tried to fight back, Desmond reached down to his holster and ripped his gun right out. With that, he launched himself back into the wall, putting as much distance between them as he could. There, he held the service pistol out, the wrong end aimed at the officer.

"You son of a bitch..." The man growled.

Desmond didn't respond, only kept it pointed. The last time he had been in this situation, it hadn't ended well. This time, he had no intent of shooting his target and he most certainly hoped that he wasn't another bulletproof freak. He stopped his arm from trembling. He saw the deputy reach for his receiver.

"You can do that." He spoke up coolly. "But is the sheriff going to do you much good when you're already dead?" He hoped his bluff didn't appear too obvious. The deputy froze and they glared at one another, two immovable objects with too much distance for Desmond to be rushed. One of them had to relent sooner or later. He may have had time working against him, but he had his unpredictability in his favour.

Eventually, one man broke. It was not Desmond. The deputy returned his arms to his sides gormlessly.

"Good." Desmond heaved. "Now, you're going to back up, slowly, and you're going to let me walk out of here. You're going to count down three minutes before you even think of calling for help."

"R-Right…" He could tell just from the Deputy's voice that his throat had run dry. That made two of them. Gently, he complied, the pair moving in an almost dance-like rhythm until Desmond was mostly out into the corridor. There, he kept the gun trained and carefully backed down towards the exit.

"You aren't gonna get away with this." The deputy decided to call out when Desmond was about halfway to the exit. "You'll be on the run for, what, a couple days tops? Once you're back here, you'll just have added charges on top of charges."

"I really - and I'm being entirely frank here - do not care." Was Desmond's response.

He never would have thought that breaking out of jail would be so easy. He supposed that wonders could arise when one's adversaries were a small-time sheriff and his portly assistant. Regardless, it was without resistance that he came out into the morning. It was bitter outside. Not raining, not quite, but obviously close to it. The skies were a clouded, swirling grey, the whole world cold and uninviting. Coming out into the fresh air for the first time in several days, he blinked once or twice. Then, he shook his head and ran.

He had but one destination in mind and no time that could go to waste.

His issued plimsolls slapped against the pavement as he sprinted, for once thankful that Greenrock had become so deserted; Were he in New York, being a man in inmate garb running down the street was probably a significantly harder feat to get away with. He could at least count his blessings on that much.

His run took him past the church. Perhaps one of the tallest buildings in the town, which wasn't exactly a massive achievement, it stood above all else and, strangely, appeared almost untouched by the cancer that had spread through the rest of Greenrock. Close inspection would reveal the stains on the windows and weeds capturing the flower boxes, but otherwise, it very much seemed as if the Lord was protecting it.

A few people, dressed severely in dark colours, were gathered around the front, a jolt to Desmond's memory as to what the day was. He slowed to a brisk jog as he realised. October Thirty-First. Exactly seventeen years since O'Connor's spree.

In the future, when he had time to look back and reflect on matters, he would say that there was something rather prophetic about all of that, as if it was all coming to a head on such a day on purpose.

Still, the amount of people, which was small but still notable, wasn't exactly something he needed right at that moment, so he made the decision to duck behind the groundskeeper's hut just adjacent to the church, nearly flattening his body to the jagged stone wall and taking a moment to regain his breath. He hunched over, going to place both hands on his knees, and that was when he realised that he was still holding the deputy's gun. It was cold to the touch, heavy as a lead block. Only with that did the enormity of things start to sink in. He must have been insane. Or determined. Probably both.

Panting gently, he took the gun and slipped it into the back waistband of his trousers, before lifting up the top and draping it over the firearm in some attempt to keep it concealed. He got the feeling that he didn't want to get rid of it just yet, but he certainly wasn't in the mood for holding it.

"Mister Ford?"

The voice caught his attention and he snapped his head up desperately to see her - *Alice,* he had to remind himself - appearing around the corner.

For a second, the pair stared at each other. Then, Desmond let out a bitter laugh, spurred on by his exhaustion and panic. "Fancy that..."

"What are you..." Slowly, yet without hesitation, she wheeled herself over to him. "I heard about the arrest. Roger said it was just as well."

Desmond chuckled through his nostrils. "And does Roger know you're talking to me right now?"

"I excused myself, told him I was going to the restroom." She explained simply. "I've probably got a few minutes before I have to get back."

Desmond brought up his hands, ran them through his hair. "You're surprisingly calm about this. You do realise I just broke out of jail?"

Alice shrugged half-heartedly. "I think enough weird things have happened in my life that I'm just not questioning it, anymore."

"Heh." He wasn't sure why, but he was suddenly overwhelmed by a desire to talk to her, to reconnect in some small way. A longing desire that thought with his common sense that dictated the necessity to get a move on. "How is that life, then?"

"Could be worse. I write poetry now, you know. Newspapers, couple of pieces for galleries. Not much, but it helps to pay the bills."

"Well, you always were the creative type." Desmond murmured back.

"I don't suppose I could write anything to get you out of this."

A coy smirk twisted on his stubbled lips. "Probably not." He looked her down. This was entirely new for him. It felt like the first conversation he had enjoyed in decades where the other party did not outright despise him. A lot had happened, but there was still some sort of warmth between them. "You know, this might all be over by tonight."

"Uh huh?" Alice enquired. "What's the plan?"

"I get in there, grab whatever I can. Documents, everything. I get out and I spread it before they kill me." He shrugged. "Easy stuff."

This got a snicker out of Alice.

"What?" He asked.

"Documents?" She sniffled. "What, do you think everything's still going into paper? We're entering a digital world, you know. Everything's on computers these days."

"You what?"

"You heard me."

That sounded absolutely absurd. "With the way that computers fail?"

"Well, they fail a lot less, now." She countered. "Especially with BLACKMATTER, they'll probably have stuff saved on their servers. I'd be surprised if there's a scrap of paper in the place."

"But wait..." This was all very sudden. "What the hell do I do, then? Carry the computers out?"

Another snicker from Alice. "You could try..." She lingered on her sentence, as if she was debating what she was about to say next. Her lips pursed and unpursed as her eyes took on a cloudy look. "I'll tell you what..." She reached into the purse slung over her chair.

"As much as I might look it, I don't think I need any lip balm." Desmond pointed out. But from her bag, Alice withdrew a portable phone. "And?"

"It's my cell." She explained, matter of factly.

"Right, I get that. But what good does that do?"

"God, you really are out of touch."

"You're enjoying this, aren't I?"

Her grin threatened to overtake most of her face. "Just a bit. Look, they can do more than call nowadays, you hear? In fact, this one here has a camera."

"A camera?" Desmond echoed. "You're joking."

"I'm not."

"In that little thing?" He tentatively took the phone and examined it. It was barely larger than his palm. "Not a chance."

"The future is now." Was Alice's reply, thinly layered with a pang of sarcasm. "Look, everything's stored on monitors, these days, so what do you do? You take the camera…" He brought her hand over, navigating his fingers to the buttons that allowed him to access said camera. "... And you snap enough pictures to use as evidence. You can carry all these out and it isn't even close to as cumbersome as a bunch of files. Isn't 2009 wonderful?"

"Well, would you look at that?" Desmond mumbled, holding out the compact little camera. Doctor Who is alive and real."

"In a sense." Alice looked hurriedly over her shoulder, as if spying for anyone who may be trying to listen in on the wheelchair-bound outsider talking to the escaped felon. "That's on the house, by the way. It's my spare. Might as well be used for some good." With a little sigh, she glanced up at the grey skies. Only then, did Desmond become aware that the elements were starting to pick up. Very few light droplets of rain pinged down from on high, without much effect. "So, you're really going ahead with this."

"Really." He confirmed.

Alice gave a small intake of breath through her teeth, a dull whistle resonating. "They'll kill you."

"Probably."

"And it doesn't bother you at all."

For just a second, Desmond closed his eyes and angled his chin upwards, letting the sparse drops of water relax upon his face. "I'll be honest, I'm getting kind of sick of saying this, of thinking this, but... I don't give much of a damn. Whatever happens to me, as long as it cripples them, is fine by me."

"Right." She nodded, as if still processing the words. "That's… Weirdly noble."

"I try." He didn't correct her, he had not the heart, but he felt the urge to contradict her. There wasn't much noble about this; He was just honouring his promise.

"Try to keep yourself alive, okay?"

"I'll give it my best try." He responded. Looking down at Alice, he sighed gently. There was something that still had to be said. "I don't think I ever told you this, but I'm sorry. Sorry about everything."

For a moment, it was impossible to gauge the woman's reaction. Her face was a mask of blankness, eyes invisible behind the lenses of her fogged-up spectacles. Her hands rested on the arm rests of her chair, fingers coiling on the edge.

"It's alright." She finally said. "What happened is in the past. For me it is, at least. I get your intentions. And that's the important part, right?"

"Right…" With that, Desmond pushed away from the wall. "In that case, I'll see you around?"

"See you around." Alice confirmed. "Even if it takes to the next life."

He took one last look at her. Then, he walked past her and left the area, not taking another look back. All things considered, he was glad for that conversation. It was something he had not realised he needed.

Now, it was time to turn his focus to the task at hand.

It was time, finally, to stick it to BLACKMATTER, and their stuffed shirt attorneys and their bizarre unkillable henchmen.

Nine

The BLACKMATTER facility looked about the same as it had when he had last left it. Shrouded in the grey of the skies above, it cast a familiarly daunting shadow upon the land surrounding it, in spite of its rather underwhelming height above the surface. The fencing was still, obviously in place, although as Desmond quickly uncovered, there was one exception.

The gate was hanging open. Someone was in the process of going through it. The very someone who probably owned the car resting on the curb a little while down the road, an old beaten up Honda that he had observed on his way up. If nothing else, this at least meant that he wouldn't have to worry about getting back in.

Drawing the gun, just in case, Desmond kept his body low and his movements quick yet quiet, as he crossed the field towards the door. He managed to reach it before it swung shut and, as he kept it propped open with his bad hand, he used the good one to press the gun directly into the back of the person. They froze up in an instant, their body jolting and going rather still as he kept the barrel pushed deep into them. He wasn't going to give them a chance to wriggle.

"Move up a bit, why don't you?" He advised. "I'd quite like to get in."

"Ford." The person realised, a voice dripping with distaste. "So the rat isn't back in his sewer yet." In an instant, he knew who it was.

"Paul." He responded. "Long time."

Paul Stanton remained steely as he complied with the command to move forwards. Desmond followed after, allowing the gate to swing shut behind him. "I rather hoped that you were finally put down." He noted, in that nostalgic, pretentious voice of his.

"And I rather hoped you were long out of the way." Desmond retorted. "How old are you now, sixty-five? And you're still minding this craphole."

"A job is a job." Stanton answered briskly. "Or have the years in prison erased your mind of honest work?"

"Sure, honest. Human experimentation, honest stuff."

"You didn't seem to have a problem with it back then."

Desmond could tell that Stanton knew his words had impact. He opened his mouth to reply, then shut it again, pressing the gun just a little harder. "Shall we go for a dander, then?"

"I don't suppose I have a choice."

Together, the pair made their way into the reception lobby of the facility and from there, towards the elevators. They took to the leftmost and Stabton drew his hand into his coat pocket. Desmond's finger tightened instinctively on the trigger, then loosened again as he saw the key card brought out. All it took was a simple swipe and after a moment's wait, the doors parted with a soft, mechanical hiss of hydraulics. The two stepped in, Stanton first of course.

Once he was safely in the lift and kept his gun aimed, Desmond leaned over and clicked the button for the lowest level, for he recalled plainly that this was where the majority of the work had gone down. The tight little metal box rattled uncomfortably and from there, they were descending, granting to him that old hated feeling of uneasiness in his legs. Something about his stomach had never handled lifts well.

"Seventeen years." He muttered aloud, taking his mind off the motion sickness. "And you've kept on slaving away down here. You and the worker bees."

"Mostly me." Stanton retorted, a clear note of detestation in his voice. "We have a skeleton crew down here. I've been heading operations down here."

"Honest work, as you said."

"Yes. Honest work. Honest work that will change the world."

"For better or for worse."

Stanton's eyes moved to glance over his back at Desmond. "You're a Goddamned idiot, Ford. Setbacks happen, and you just had to blow your top."

"I'm not the one who insisted we continue with an unstable project." He pointed out.

"Jackass. Using O'Connor was a fool's move." Stanton actually scoffed. "A veteran, what the hell were they thinking? We always knew we needed someone made of stronger stuff. Subjects who wouldn't be so susceptible."

Suddenly, Desmond was quietly fighting the urge to shoot Stanton then and there. "Lunatics really do find any excuse to sound justified."

"Pot, meet kettle." Stanton sneered. "I'm not a murderer, Ford: In fact, it may interest you to know that we haven't had a single fatality since '92. Because we learned, we didn't repeat our mistakes. Are you aware of that concept?"

Desmond didn't reply. Thankfully, he did not need to, for at that point, the descent stopped and the doors pursed themselves open. Pointing Stanton out first, he followed out into the corridor that waited.

Now, this was more like it. In stark contrast to the public levels of the facility, down below was clean, well lit with overhead white, clearly inhabited and used. It was like stepping into a totally different world from what he had already seen of the facility and Greenrock as a whole.

Unlike everywhere else, down here had not changed.

"Brings you back, doesn't it?" Stanton noted snidely as he was urged down the corridor and towards the main area of the level.

Desmond kept silent. The last time that he had traced this journey, it had been under far different circumstances. The path that led him to Acker's murder, the path that would change the outcome of, certainly, his own life. It was somewhat hard to lament though, with Stanton continuing to goad.

"Plenty of us left, of course. After what you did. Lorde, he got together with Lucy Wallace. They're together over in California now. Mulligan left, Trevors transferred up to the D.C. offices. Only a few of us stayed. Only a few of us continued the dream. BLACKMATTER's chosen doctors."

"You talk too much, Paul." Desmond finally muttered, even as he continued to relive the nightmare of that day in his head. "Without saying anything at all."

It was as if he was tracing his exact steps, one by one. He wasn't sure if this was intentional to some subconscious degree or not. He tried not to think about it, as they turned the corner and drew closer to their ultimate destination.

"If only you could see the leaps and bounds we've made." Stanton started up again. "Over the last decades. Maybe, if you'd seen what we have now, you'd have found some sense. We're beyond just arms now. So, so far beyond."

"And it's all still using that chip?" Desmond couldn't stop himself from asking. The bitterness was evident in his voice.

Stanton sighed, as if he were dealing with a child. "A far evolved version, but yes, that is the basic gist. Acker would have loved it. Had you not murdered her, of course."

Once again, no response. He kept his lips safely clamped, as he moved up, came to a heavy set door and moved right through it wordlessly.

And just like that, he was in.

All the way back. The main laboratory floor also hadn't changed much in all of those years. The main difference was that now, it was far more packed. Machinery lined the sides, everything that Desmond recognised in an updated capacity and a fair few things that he could not even hope to comprehend. It also appeared somewhat bigger, but that could have been a mere trick of his mind. Overhead, an observation balcony looked over the whole thing, from which one could see all down below.

For just a moment, he could have sworn that he saw a chalk outline on the pristine marble flooring; A blink confirmed this to be a trick of his eyes.

"I'll take your silence for astonishment." Stanton muttered sarcastically as he was pushed further into the room. "You may have killed Acker, but the project didn't die with her. Hell, it didn't even kill our funding by much."

Desmond remained quiet as he lamented to himself on how insane that was. Two major incidents in the space of twenty-four hours had been caused by Icarus back in 1992, how in the hell had it not impacted things at all? Perhaps Price's talk of friends in high places was less posturing than initially suspected. Shaking his head, he readjusted his thoughts, pointing up to the observation deck with his eyes.

"Let's take a walk up there, shall we?" He wanted to get out of there as soon as possible. And he was fairly certain that there were computers up there.

Sure enough, there were. Pushing Stanton over to them, Desmond gave a muttered command for him to log in. As usual, the doctor complained, nothing unusual there, but did get onto it, eventually, entering in his details under threat of death. One nice thing about having a reputation as a murderer was that people tended to take one's threats seriously. Desmond had learned this in prison, and it was certainly coming into effect now.

"You won't get far with this." Stanton couldn't help but sneer. "I can see what you're planning here. No paper would be insane enough to take your story. Even if they were, you aren't getting out of here. Not when *he* arrives."

Desmond had a fairly good idea who *he* was, but he reasoned to cross that bridge when he came to it. "How about you just do your job, alright, Paul?"

With plenty more grumbling, Stanton did just that, and before long, the system was up and running. "Emails." Desmond urged; He reckoned that they would be the easiest source to snap a few pictures of.

He obeyed and before long, both men were staring down a rather vast inbox. All kinds of names were there. Felicity Trevors, James Pegorino, even the name Alex Moore, whom even the out of touch Desmond recognised as a name belonging to a senator.

"Moore?" He whistled. "How deep does this thing go?"

"Deeper than you could ever imagine." Stanton replied.

Desmond shrugged this off and, using his wrist to awkwardly keep the gun pressed into Stanton's back, he read through some of the emails. Much of it was hard to decipher, written in double entendres and various other irritating codes, but he was getting the message. There was a lot to read into. In particular, talks of test subjects, victims of the Icarus Project.

"Like rats..." He muttered. "You people didn't learn from O'Connor in the slightest..." That disgust was starting to hone itself, becoming far more pronounced. "All that talk of past mistakes..."

"We never used someone as unstable as that again." Was Stanton's retort. "These people are thoroughly vetted. Might I remind you that we've had no incidents since then. No incidents, no deaths."

"And how much, exactly, have these people consented?" Desmond spat; Stanton didn't reply.

Overtaken in a sudden fit of rage, he slammed his former colleague's head into the desk, then held it there as he used his good hand to draw out the phone and take as many photographs as he could. Addresses, contents, he snapped and he snapped until he was sure that he had reached the limit of the poor phone's memory. He hoped that it was enough. It probably was. With a bit of luck, there would be somebody out there who was insane enough to do something with them. He reasoned in his mind that he could ask Alice for some sort of assistance on that end, recalling her words about having some of her works published in papers.

"You've been a wonderful help…" He grunted with thickly layer sarcasm as he returned the phone to his pocket and regained his tighter grip on the gun, allowing Stanton to get back up. "Maybe with a bit of luck, I won't be the only one facing down a legal storm soon."

Stanton did not reply to this; He simply looked over the balcony's railings and nodded, satisfied. Then, he spoke.

Not to Desmond.

"Carter." He stated. "Glad to see you."

"Huh?" Caught off-guard by this, Desmond too looked down to the main laboratory floor. And who he saw standing down there, black suit and all, an expression as emotionless as ever and his own gun in hand, was the stalker.

"Damn." He muttered. And then, it sank in and he tilted his head curiously. "Carter?"

"I think you might want to take me down to him." Stanton replied simply. "I'm sure you don't want him coming up here."

All at once, Desmond pieced it together. He realised what seemed so familiar about the stalker. He was certainly older, taller and slimmer, but that face was one, even with dark glasses, that he could recognise. Old Bobby Carter, former security officer for the premises.

"Christ above…" He groaned, fairly certain that his face was going a sheet white as he spoke.

"Surprised?" He could hear the grin on Stanton's lips. "This is like a regular little reunion."

Ten

The journey down to the main floor felt as if it took a century. Gently, carefully, Desmond descended those twisting steps, making sure to keep that pistol rammed into the unusually quiet Stanton's back at all times. His mind was alight with potential solutions to this, even as he continued to reel from the reveal of Carter's identity. Whatever had happened to him, bullets clearly were not going to work - that still sounded so absurd to think of in his head - and he didn't reckon that he was going to be able to walk out of this one easily. All he had was a hostage. One single bargaining chip.

"You know…" Stanton unfortunately spoke up again as they reached the final few steps. "Your biggest mistake, Ford, aside from not curling up and dying in jail? It was calling me." He appeared to barely restrain himself from spitting. "How stupid can you be? I knew you were up to something the moment I got that Goddamned call. So, I put in a few words to the top brass…"

"And they sent Bobby in." Desmond realised through grit teeth. He wasn't going to actively admit it, of course, but he couldn't escape the feeling that Stanton had a point, that the stalker had been dispatched because of his decision, what seemed like an age ago now, to contact Stanton on his first day back in Greenrock.

"In short. He's looking good for himself, wouldn't you agree? He, my friend, is the walking embodiment of Icarus. A true masterpiece. And wouldn't you know, he hasn't gone mad?"

Desmond felt the spitting urge to retort with "You've done enough of that for anybody here."

Coming out into the main floor, they were greeted with the sight of Carter standing right there. Well-built, tall, a far cry from his past self. It was starting to make a lot more sense. Desmond made sure to keep Stanton in between himself and Carter. He came a few feet away and stopped, tightening his grip on his hostage.

After a moment, Carter was the first to speak. "You had your chance." He stated gravely. "Plenty of them."

"That I did, Bobby." Desmond replied. "It's good to see you again."

Carter gave no reaction to this, keeping his gun pointed. "My job is to prevent anybody from compromising BLACKMATTER's position here in Greenrock." Briefly, Desmond wondered why.

"You have the Icarus chip, don't you?"

No answer.

After a second, Stanton provided one. "We've gone so far beyond prosthetic limbs. Try a prosthetic body."

"Mad science at its finest…" Desmond muttered.

"Madly brilliant, maybe." Was Stanton's clipped reply. "Now, I rather reckon that you would do well to let go of me. You're making matters more complicated than they need be with this pathetic charade. Why don't you play a man's game and face your maker with some dignity?"

"I have no intention of dying tonight." Desmond's grasp only grew tighter, the gun pushed that bit deeper into Stanton's back.

"Well, that just makes you an even greater fool." Stanton glared over at Carter. "You know your job. Get it over with."

Carter didn't speak. He kept his gun aimed and fired.

The crack of the pistol deafened Desmond as the muzzle flash blinded him. Flesh tore and blood spurted up, coating the floor.

Desmond stayed standing. He felt no pain. What he did feel was Stanton buckling in his grasp.

The only noise was the sound of dripping as blood filtered out of the wound in Stanton's chest and splashed on the flooring, staining its otherwise perfect cleanliness.

When Stanton spoke again, his voice trembled. "What the hell…"

Carter was unfazed. "Sorry. As I said, my job is to remove any obstacles that could negatively impact BLACKMATTER. You allowed Doctor Ford access to the system."

Desmond released his hold on Stanton, letting the man fell forward onto his knees, grasping his wound. "You stupid prick!" He yelped, voice on the edge of sobs.

Carter fired again. A crimson fountain cascaded out of the back of Stanton's head, splattering Desmond behind him, and he collapsed, with a few more limp twitches before falling still.

And that was that, as far as Paul Stanton was concerned.

"God…" Desmond muttered. As much as it may have only been his second murder seen close up, that didn't make matters any better. He still felt sick to his stomach.

In no time at all, the gun was raised and pointed at him. He acted fast and without much forethought, squeezing the trigger of his own weapon.

Nothing. It didn't even fire.

Cursing, he threw his body behind a particularly large bit of machinery, purely hoping to put a decent bit of distance between himself and Carter, at least enough to block any incoming shots. The room came alive with the gunfire as the assailant took a few potshots, prompting Desmond down to the ground as he gripped his head, all the while trying to figure out the gun. It had to be loaded, right? There was no reason why an officer of the law wouldn't keep it as such in his mind. That entirely defeated the purpose. He hit the damned thing off the side of the machine he was crouched behind, for all the good that it did him.

The footsteps were heavy and concrete, and sheer panic gripped Desmond, forcing him away from his cover and into a frantic dash towards the doors. He had come too close now. Too close to die. He hunched as he ran, trying to minimise his size as much as possible. Two more shots travelled over his head, managing to miss him by some absurd miracle.

Reaching the door, he charged right through it, coming into the corridor and taking a sharp left turn towards where the elevator had been. He ran faster than he probably ever had in his life, feeling the sharp pain of the stitch worming its way into both of his sides. Sweat plastered his hair down firmly to his scalp like a thick adhesive. He didn't even once look behind, he just pelted ahead at full speed. Not that he needed to look, the footsteps told him more than enough.

Another gunshot and the pain shot up through Desmond as if he had been struck by a bolt from Zeus. It took him only moments to ascertain that he had been shot in the ankle, as he collapsed like a startled gazelle blood seeped through the leg of his trousers, darkening the blue fabric as he twisted. Behind him, Carter was approaching and preparing to fire yet again, the shot that would end it all.

Glancing back to where he was intending to run to, he saw the lift to be so very close, barely out of his range. So, with flailing motions like a fish trapped on land, he spun and he writhed and he forced himself up, sprinting for the lift even as the pain threatened to split him apart entirely.

He made it in, launching himself against the back wall of the elevator and desperately slamming the button that would send him up back to the surface, those footsteps the orchestra for his demise. At what felt like an agonisingly slow rate, those doors appeared to close. Then, they snapped shut, blocking out the sights of what had been beyond.

Desmond knew he shouldn't fall into complacency just yet, but he could not prevent a long, relieved sigh as, still gripping the gun so tight that his knuckles paled, he leaned back on the wall and cast his eyes up.

The celebrations came too early.

With a lurch of buckling metal, even as the lift was beginning to move, those doors were forced all the way open, pried apart like weak aluminium under the heavy arms of Carter.

Panic flashed through him. As if desperate to do something, anything at all, he raised his gun and squeezed the trigger again and again, even as he knew it to be an entirely fruitless endeavour. Then, it struck him.

The safety.

Cursing his own stupidity in forgetting such a thing, he quickly found and released what he hoped to be the safety latch as Carter began to pull himself into the elevator. He didn't know what it was going to achieve, but maybe he could manage something.

So, he fired. He fired into Carter's chest. Not a thing. Then, his hip. Still nothing, just a slight stagger at most. Then, he aimed his third, surely pointless shot at the man's left arm. Once again, it was of little consequence, but he saw it quiver for just a second, and saw the door slide a little further shut.

That was it. That had to be his sole remaining hope.

So, Desmond fired. He sent shot after shot into that arm, hoping to destabilise it just enough. After just four shots, he saw the forearm tremble and just like that, for only a second, Carter lost his grip.

As the door slid shut, Desmond's stalker attempted to pull his body right through before it did so, but he was to only get halfway. The doors clamped shut around his waist and as the lift rose up, the top of the frame was then pushing down on him as well. For a few seconds, the lift was held in place; Then, it all gave way. With the guttural screeching of shattered metal, Bobby Carter was split right down the waist. His front half fell into the elevator, as everything below the stomach slid out and disappeared from view. The elevator continued rising as if nothing had happened.

Desmond was left gasping and panting, his heart just about ready to burst out of his chest, as he flattened his hand to his body, dropping the gun with a resounding clang. So, was that it, then?

Incredulous, he looked over. With it split open like a cross-section, he could see the mechanical parts that made up Bobby Carter. An entirely prosthetic body. Just as Stanton had said. Curiosity taking a hold of him, Desmond kneeled down and pulled back his collar. Sure enough, lodged on the back of his neck, there it was.

The Icarus chip. The little thing that had caused so much strife in the last two decades. The ultimate child of BLACKMATTER and Acker's research. A neural interface that would allow a person to directly control prosthetics as if they were flesh and blood. Amputees would virtually be a thing of the past. He had to give Stanton one thing, the project had the power to change the world. But the consequences? O'Connor's chip had malfunctioned, driven him into a frenzy. Such a thing was entirely unacceptable and that BLACKMATTER continued with the project after that was, in his mind, downright criminal.

Acker was the same. When he looked at it from an outside perspective, he couldn't entirely say that he blamed her. Penny was paralysed. The thought of her daughter ever being able to walk must have been too alluring for the doctor to bear. So, she had carried on. And Desmond had killed her for it. He would not allow for Penny to meet the same fate as O'Connor. That was what had really kickstarted everything.

The journey up to the surface felt to take an age, certainly not helped in any respect whatsoever by the fact that he was sharing his transportation with a seemingly unconscious and apparently nigh-unkillable former colleague of his (a statement that he didn't believe he would ever be making within any realm of reality), but it did eventually reach its conclusion, as the lift halted with another lurch and the doors slid open.

His hair plastered down and his pores wide open, allowing the waves of sweat to drip down his face, pooling at his chin, Desmond stepped towards the doors. He was barely a fraction of the way there when he was grabbed.

Carter's hand kept a tight hold on his ankle, squeezing it as if it were an orange he was particularly intent on extracting the juice from, continuing even as he lacked a lower body. Desmond's response was immediate, before the panic could fully settle in; He brought down the gun and pulled the trigger once more.

Empty. Of course.

That aforementioned panic beginning to worm its way in, he tossed the weapon at Carter, expecting very little to arise from that and receiving exactly what he had anticipated. Still, the grip only tightened as he was dragged towards the dismembered hunter.

"For God's sake…" He growled. Had this farce not gone on for long enough yet? Precisely how much more of this could he even take? His already present limp worsened, the blood from the gunshot wound spurting over and drooling over Carter's mechanical hand.

Carter didn't speak. He retained a single-minded determination for nothing else than rooting out and destroying the source of the problem, in his mind. This was who he was now.

Matters only worsened, as Carter thrust his other hand up to Desmond's hip and started to haul his body up, resilient to the latter's attempts to throw him off. Only as he crawled up like a fungus did Desmond truly appreciate the weight of this prosthetic body of his, the weight that he found himself careening to the ground over. On the way down, he slammed his head on the side of the lift.

Everything seemed to swim. He couldn't even feel the pain that was surely developing in his head, nor could he see a thing through the blurry mess that was made of his vision by a collective of tears and strain. He was pinned, and Carter was now on top of him. What came next was only the logical way to proceed.

Desmond felt as those cold hands coiled themselves around his throat, closing tight on them and crushing any gap that allowed oxygen to pass. Desmond spluttered, choking up a storm as he felt his energy drain like juice from an extractor. Half-delirious, he saw a thousand different images bouncing around his view, unable to even take in most of it.

The already blurred indifference that was his vision was beginning to blacken. Faint gasps of air were taken, but barely any was entering his lungs. Through the haze, he could just about make out Carter's face, but not read the emotions on it, if there were indeed any at all.

This was to be it.

So close, and yet, so very far. One more body on the pile. Andrew O'Connor, Sarah Acker, Paul Stanton, Desmond Ford. Maybe, in some twisted sense, he could be the last.

...

No. That was absurd and even as broken-minded as he was, he knew it. Things were not going to change. BLACKMATTER's experimentation would not end, the lives of those lured in as subjects for their games would not be exalted. Everything would just carry on as normal, sans two more people involved in the matter. Things weren't ever going to improve.

Not unless the truth got out. If it ever did get out.

Who else could ensure that?

In a sense, Desmond invoked a similar reaction to what he had felt earlier at the jail, summoning a sudden bout of strength through pure tenacity, a burst of acknowledgement that shot through his entire system, screaming in his ear that the job had to be done. In one last attempt, he thrust both hands up and gripped Carter's head, trying his best to twist it to the side, to throw him off course. It felt fleshy, human. There was one part of the man that had not been made artificial, clearly. But Desmond paid that hardly any heed, as he pushed back the head, even as the hands remained tightly on his throat. He grit his teeth, the blood flowing through his system and hammering in his ears as he pushed it as far as he could. One hand, his bad hand, slipped, leaving a trail of blood across Carter's lower jaw, and as it did so, he flailed his fingers wildly. They dusted the edge of the chip on the back of his neck.

Renewed, Desmond tried again, using his bad hand to push the head back as his good reached around the neck for the chip. He swiped at it once, twice, then got a hold on his third attempt. With that, he pulled with all of his might.

For the first time, Carter showed emotion. A visceral, guttural howl of legitimate pain as Desmond ripped the chip right off the back of his neck with one hasty motion. He snapped back, his entire remaining body convulsed, the grip on Desmond's neck loosened and all seemed to fall very still.

Gasping against the elevator's wall, Desmond slowly felt his senses start to return with him. His vision came first, still clouded, but at least, in some sense, functional enough to observe the scene ahead of him. Carter lay on the ground just a few paces in front, his face locked in an eternal, silent screech, his spine arched back as thin red droplets oozed from the back of his neck. On the floor by his side, there lay the Icarus Chip. A tiny, little implant that had caused so much damage.

It took another half minute or so for Desmond to regain enough of his senses to bring himself up to his feet, almost collapsing right away as he put too much force on his botched ankle. There, in the now-silent lift he stood, glancing down at Carter. Looking at it, he wasn't too sure what had done him in for good. Maybe it was the shock, maybe the pain, or maybe his mechanical body provided some sort of life support. Desmond didn't know and he didn't really care anymore. With one last look at the former security guard, he stepped over the body and went out into the lobby.

He felt... He wasn't quite sure how he felt, actually. Exhausted, in undeniable pain... relieved, maybe? The feeling of a two decade long chapter of one's life reaching its end was certainly a momentous one. With small, deliberate movements, he inched towards the door, through which streamed the natural grey light from the outside world. For Greenlock, the world was still as grey and overcast as ever.

For Desmond, it felt just that little bit brighter.

Epilogue

When Desmond Ford left the BLACKMATTER facility that day, it was the last time he would ever be in Greenrock.

Prior to his departure, he visited the Baxters' temporary residence, gave Alice the phone with the photographs. Just a few days later, a wide variety of local, state and national news sources would find emails from a mystery whistleblower. These emails came from a freshly created account that had never been used for anything else and was deactivated by its user a week after sending out the messages.

It took a while to bite, most discredited it as a prank, but eventually one did not. A particularly enthusiastic young journalist for the *Arkansas Democrat-Gazette* decided to humour the allegations towards BLACKMATTER and, somehow, managed to get it published.

From there, it was like one big domino effect. More and more sources began to pick up on the story, it started to spread across the country like a plague. By late November, BLACKMATTER's illicit research had become the Watergate of the 2000s.

Eventually, the Federal Bureau of Investigation organised a raid on BLACKMATTER's Greenrock facility. They found the majority of the systems and files to have been wiped, but the thing with electronics is that there was always a paper trail. They managed to recover a few basic receipts, implicating the company on a national scale, and so the dominos kept falling.

Friends in high places can do a lot to stave off private investigations, but once the public is aware of a conspiracy? The police essentially had no choice but to investigate. Questions were asked, buildings were raided. Heads were about to roll.

The first sign of the whole house coming down was when BLACKMATTER president Carl Leary stepped down from his position in March of 2010. He quietly retired to the Bahamas and had not been seen since. His replacement made lip service to setting the record straight, but that meant little good. They were gearing towards a coverup.

In April, Felicity Trevors, who had spearheaded the Icarus Project after Acker's death from Washington D.C, simply disappeared right off the face of the earth. The official story was that she had decided to flee amidst the controversy. She was not the only BLACKMATTER associate to fall into this category.

Not all of them did, though. The company's head attorney, Gerry Price, was arraigned that same month, charged with accessory to crimes against humanity, in relation to the evidence of human experimentation on the Icarus Project. Days later, Senator Alex Moore stepped down, pending an investigation into his affairs. The predators were devouring each other in a desperate bid for survival.

But for Desmond Ford? That didn't mean much of anything at all to him.

He was right back where he had started.

"Ford." One of the guards commanded as they drew close to his cell. "You've got common room time."

"Right." Slowly, Desmond stood up from his bed, brushing down his uniform. The sentence had not been kind. Twenty-five years for a combination of his parole violation, theft, illegal use of a firearm and the assault on an officer. That essentially cemented that the rest of his life was to be spent behind bars. But he didn't particularly care. That was of no more concern to him. He had been keeping up with the news and he knew for a fact that he had, somehow, managed to rise against his odds. BLACKMATTER was collapsing. Was there any sweeter tune?

Approaching the door, he took a look at his desk, where rested the letter and enclosed poem that Alice had sent him. He was still intending to get around to writing back to her; He told himself that he would do it sooner or later.

He allowed himself to be released from the cell and, guards behind him, headed down towards the common room. It was quiet. Oddly quiet. One could usually expect the clanging of chains and general moaning of his fellow inmates, but on this day, it was downright peaceful. Odd. Not that he was complaining. He appreciated a bit of quiet for once.

Coming to the open doorway that led into the common room, he peeked inside. There were a few other prisoners already in there. Some were watching the television, others playing table tennis. But he knew for a fact that something was off. None of them appeared focused on their activities. There was a sense of underlying tension, as if they were waiting for something - or someone - else.

He looked to one of the guards, who shrugged noncommittally. "We'll be keeping an eye on things." He advised as he stepped back and allowed Desmond to enter the room.

So, this was it, then. Maybe he was being paranoid, but it seemed somewhat unlikely.

Was he happy with how he had handled things? Acker, his whole quest to expose BLACKMATTER?

Not exactly. But he had done it. Now, that was all that mattered. He had made his decisions, and he accepted where it had all led.

Without fear in his heart and with his head held high, Desmond entered the common room, ready for what awaited.

A flower unheeded, shall wilt and die,
Alone, without water, care or the skies,
In a gardener's hands, so tender, so fair,
That flower can sprout, can love and can care.

Extract from New Blood,
Penelope A. Baxter